Anxious Hearts

"The blustery landscapes and
their intimate connection
to the characters' plight are
reminiscent . . . of certain
scenes spent in seaside forests
by a similarly thwarted
vampire/human teen couple."
—*School Library Journal*

a novel by
TUCKER SHAW

PRAISE FOR

....

"This plot structure is quite seamless in execution. Eva's voice keeps the book grounded in modern sensitivities. Like Longfellow, Shaw gives nature high importance through descriptive passages of his chosen Maine setting and pays homage in many other small ways from incorporating original lines into dialogue and transplanting subtleties of characters' personalities. He is in no way, however, a slave to Longfellow, delivering both a couple of steamier scenes and potential for happiness in the end. The blustery landscapes and their intimate connection to the characters' plight are reminiscent . . . of certain scenes spent in seaside forests by a similarly thwarted vampire/human teen couple. It is this very power to evoke both admired historical fiction and hot teen literature that will prove this novel's success." —*School Library Journal*

"The mirrored yet divergent plot lines underline the similarities between ancient and contemporary romances, and suspense builds into a slight twist at the end." —*Publishers Weekly*

"Shaw's creative telling of these dual sagas will keep the reader turning pages." —*ALAN Review*

ALSO BY
TUCKER SHAW
The Girls

Anxious Hearts

a novel by

TUCKER SHAW

AMULET BOOKS
NEW YORK

The Library of Congress has cataloged the hardcover edition as follows:

Shaw, Tucker.
Anxious hearts / by Tucker Shaw.
p. cm.
Summary: In alternate chapters, retells events of Henry Wadsworth Longfellow's poem "Evangeline," and relates a modern-day tale of Maine teens who were childhood friends and later grew to love each other, and who, when pulled apart, are determined to reunite.
ISBN 978-0-8109-8718-0
[1. Love—Fiction. 2. Acadians—Fiction. 3. High schools—Fiction. 4. Schools—Fiction. 5. Nova Scotia—History—1713–1763—Fiction. 6. Maine—Fiction.] I. Longfellow, Henry Wadsworth, 1807–1882. Evangeline. II. Title.
PZ7.S53445Anx 2010
[Fic]—dc22
2009039754

Paperback ISBN 978-0-8109-9711-0

Amulet Books are available at special discounts when purchased in quantity for premiums and promotions as well as fundraising or educational use. Special editions can also be created to specification. For details, contact specialmarkets@abramsbooks.com or the address below.

ABRAMS
THE ART OF BOOKS SINCE 1949
115 West 18th Street
New York, NY 10011
www.abramsbooks.com

*This book is for my grandmother, Barbara Shaw,
who sees a story everywhere she looks*

Prologue

Look around.

Behind you the forest is thick, gray-green and silent and dark. Craggy pine trees stand in crowded clusters, shading the mossy ground with pointed shadows. Shafts of fizzy daylight dribble through the canopy onto the cushion of leafy undergrowth, dispersing into a pulsing green glow.

You stand at the edge of the wood, on a path that cuts faintly through the bearberry bushes and the ivory grove of birch trees. A deliberate path, but obscured, half hidden by undergrowth and fallen hemlocks. Where does it lead?

You follow this path, this stony stream, through a carpet of scarlet and yellow wood lilies as it curls out of the woods and into a billowy meadow of golden-green beach grass. The air, now a salty mist, carries a quiet, far-off rumble, the groan of the distant ocean tides.

This path, like all paths and all stories, leads forward, through the calico grasses and thorny rose brambles, toward the horizon, toward the sky. But after a mile, or many, this path ends abruptly, where the ground falls away at what feels like the edge of the world. Only air, white and blue and yellow, and sea, white and blue and black, lie in front of you.

You step back from the unexpected precipice at your feet before peering warily over its edge. The cliff is vast, red-black and craggy, its narrow ledges populated by lean clusters of daredevil pine trees rooted precariously in the rock, far above the muffled waves and frothy whirlpools that snake and swirl through the rugged outcroppings a thousand feet below.

This bluff is a wild place, endless and open. You are alone here.

And yet, the air here is alive.

You trace back toward the woods, away from the cliff and into the taller grasses. There, you come upon the weathered remnants of a low wall of mossy granite, crumbling in places but solid. Beyond the wall, huddled against two hulking, primeval boulders, are the hollow remains of an ancient, neglected stone building. The structure, just big enough for a small dwelling, sits alone on this bluff, roofless and exposed, its forgotten threshold facing the open sky. Still farther on, a low rock, flat-topped and smooth, an altar, rises from the grassy ground.

In the distance, a wood bird argues with a seabird, shrill voices trilling across the meadow. The breeze strengthens and swirls, weaving through the grasses, and gathering clouds twist lazily in the sky. You lie down atop the flat rock and listen. The wind whispers, hums, groans. You stare at the every-colored sky above and listen.

Whose path was this? Whose altar? Whose story lived here?

PART ONE

eva

I hate reading.

All those words. It's painful. Give me biology. Gym. A frog to dissect. Some laps to run. Anything but English. All those words.

What have words ever done for anyone anyway? Can you catch fish with words? Can you pick berries with words? Fix a car? Heal the sick? No. Waste of time.

Especially poetry. Words that don't even make sense. And you're supposed to read them out loud. Please, tie me to a tractor. I can't wait for next year, when all I have to do is coast. Then real life takes over and, if I don't get out of Franktown, Maine, beats me senseless.

I think even Mr. Denis hates all the read-aloud stuff, even though he's a big believer in words. Or maybe he hates it *because* he's a big believer in words. He can't stand to listen to us shred them in his class.

But he pronounces things wrong, too. Like the town up the road, Calais? Mr. Denis thinks it rhymes with *ballet*. If you're from here you know that *Calais* rhymes with *Alice. Palace. Callous. Malice.*

The other thing about Mr. Denis is he doesn't like to be corrected. Mostly he just paces back and forth while we go around the room reading aloud. Today the lucky poem is "The Courtship of Miles Standish," which he thought we'd be "wicked excited about" (his words) because the guy who wrote it was from Maine, but what Mr. Denis doesn't know is that this part of Maine has nothing to do with that part of Maine. Another thing he doesn't know is that when people like him say things like "wicked excited" it sounds stupid. Wicked stupid, as a matter of fact. He also doesn't know that no high school junior is going to get excited about a two-hundred-year-old poem anyway.

Back and forth in front of the windows, Mr. Denis just paces, looking out into the fog, which hasn't lifted all day. Behind him, Louise catches my eye and makes a face. I roll my eyes, catching John Baptiste in my peripheral vision, pointing at me like he's pointing a gun, and winking. No joke. *Winking.* What a tool. I look back at my textbook.

Back and forth paces Mr. Denis, licking his finger and smoothing the last few hairs left on his head, back and forth past the rows of desks, pretending not to look at us, almost closing his eyes, then without warning spinning around with a *snap!* to try and catch someone in the act of, I don't know, passing a note I guess. Or falling asleep.

Or not paying attention, like Gabe Lejeune, who as usual is hunched over that mysterious notebook he carries around everywhere, running his left hand through his floppy chestnut hair and scribbling away with his other hand, writing whatever it is he writes in there.

I wonder what he writes about.

"Mr. Lejeune!" says Mr. Denis. "You are next."

Gabe doesn't even look up. He has no idea it's his turn to read.

Gabriel

EVANGELINE SET DOWN HER RAKE AND UNTIED her felt cloak of cornflower blue, draping it over the fence that enclosed the small garden in front of the small, square stone-and-log house. She pushed her linen sleeves up over her forearms, swiped her hair away from her face, and looked up at the low, wispy clouds above. Gabriel seized on the gesture, sweeping his charcoal across the sheet of birchbark.

No good, he thought. He tossed the birchbark sheet aside and began to sweat with frustration. He glared at his inept hand, his sloppy sketch, and fretted. What if he was never able to accomplish this task? What if he never captured Evangeline's beauty? He pulled another piece of birchbark from his foresleeve and smoothed it over his thigh.

Gabriel's failure as an artist wasn't for lack of trying. Gabriel had spent hours, days, years watching Evangeline, his bewitcher, and equal hours, days, years trying to draw her. Another eye might call his drawings fair, even beautiful, but not Gabriel. He knew they were poor. Empty. Anemic representations of the exquisite Evangeline.

Gabriel took a deep, silent breath. Perhaps he just didn't have enough skill yet. After all, no one ever showed him how to use charcoal from a dead fire to draw on sheets of birchbark. He'd discovered that himself. No one showed him the tricks of light and shape and how to convey them. But he knew. Still, he could not capture Evangeline. Nothing he created could approach her beauty.

Practice, he said to himself. This is your life's work. There is nothing else. There is *no one* else.

Gabriel and Evangeline were betrothed sixteen months now, just long enough for him to follow the custom of the Cadians and build her a home, a strong house of stone and wood aside an orchard of twelve saplings, eight apple and four pear, and a small outbuilding for goats and chickens and cider making.

Evangeline's beauty and intelligence were known throughout the Cadian lands. Her hand was coveted by every bachelor on the shores of Glosekap Bay. But Gabriel, with persistence and hopefulness and true love, had won her over all the others.

She had chosen *him*.

She does not yet belong to me, Gabriel reminded himself. Not yet. That will come tomorrow, when she becomes my wife.

Gabriel and Evangeline had played together as children, archery and footraces and blindman's bluff, as had all the children in the harborside village of Pré-du-sel. But the fastest and strongest among them were Gabriel and Evangeline. And their fathers, both widowers, were old friends.

In the years when she grew taller and he broader, their paths diverged. He took to the arts of tanning and carpentry and blacksmithing, she to the arts of spinning and farming and cider pressing. Her life was on the farm, where she cared for her aging father. His life was in the village, where he fanned the fire in his father's blacksmith shop. The games and races were left to the younger ones. Seasons went by, one following the last, the next ever approaching, and the space between the two motherless children expanded.

But in his fifteenth year, three summers ago, Gabriel saw that Evangeline, once just a playmate and companion, had transformed into a vibrant beauty.

One of those love-struck mornings, in the misty darkness

of the pre-dawn hours, Gabriel hiked to the top of Evangeline's bec. At sunrise, the mist became a drizzle and forced him to find shelter under the hang of a boulder at the edge of her apple orchard, where he curled up and, weary from the walk and the early hour, promptly fell asleep.

At midmorning, he was jostled awake with a violent prod.

"Attend!" he gasped, opening his eyes and tensing his muscles.

A blurry figure was standing over him, wrapped in a cloud of golden pink mist and pressing the blade of a garden hoe to his throat.

"What is your purpose here?" the figure demanded.

Gabriel blinked through the haze to see that his attacker was his Evangeline, his desired, illuminated with an angel's glow. "My beloved," he said, squinting up at the vision of her, straining to bring her into focus.

"What?" she said.

"Evangeline Bellefontaine," he said, surprised that the words rose so easily from his lips, even in this awkward pose. His eyes traveled across her freckled cheek to rest on the tensed ridge of her lovely jaw.

Evangeline pressed the blade of her hoe more forcefully against his neck, and her tone dropped lower. "What are you doing here, Gabriel Lajeunesse?" Evangeline said, her untamed hair dropping in heavy black waves from her perfect head. "Why are you in my father's orchard?" She tightened her grip on the hoe's handle.

"I fell asleep," Gabriel said without breathing, because he had seen the dog, the snarling, angry dog with curly black fur, at Evangeline's feet.

"Easy, Poc," she said to the dog. "Don't bite him. Not yet."

Gabriel exhaled. "I'm sorry," he said, or at least meant to say.

"You were stealing apples."

"I was stealing nothing," Gabriel said. He paused, then continued. "I am here only to breathe the ocean air that feeds your lungs while you sleep, only to receive the sounds of this windy bec that fill your ears by day." He pointed toward the stone and log home beyond the orchard, Evangeline's home, and the ocean beyond. "That I might know this place. That I might know you." He slowly rose to his elbows. "Forgive me," he said.

"Your words are foolish," she said, "but they are more considered than some." For a desperately short moment, hope washed through Gabriel. "But if you were not stealing, then you were spying," Evangeline said. She studied his face for a moment. "Your eyes tell me you are not a danger, only a nuisance." She stepped back and tucked the hoe under her arm. "A poetic nuisance, perhaps. But you must leave at once." Gabriel scrambled to his feet.

"I was not spying, Mademoiselle Bellefontaine," Gabriel said boldly. He smoothed his felt jacket and tried in vain to slick down a curled cowlick. He turned toward the path he'd hiked up.

"You'll never get home that way," she said. "The path you followed here will be impassable after this morning's rain. But if you do a task for me, I'll show you a better way."

"Anything," Gabriel answered.

And she asked him to stack firewood, and he did, great piles of it. And she fed him porridge and honey and cider. "You must never spy again," she said.

9

"I will prove my sincerity to you," he answered. "I will dedicate my life, long or short, pleasant or tragic, to this task alone."

Gabriel knew his words were grandiose, and he honored them.

It took months, years. It took bushels of pears and cords of wood and gifts of tobacco and brandy for her father, the farmer Monsieur Bellefontaine. It required assisting with the goats and gardens, and it took scaring off a pair of lynxes who cornered Poc behind Evangeline's compost pile. It took love poems whispered in the garden. But Gabriel's persistence, fueled by his soul-filling desire, won Evangeline's heart and her father's favor, above all other suitors in Pré-du-sel, including Jean-Baptiste Leblanc, the notary's son.

Gabriel turned his attention back to Evangeline, now scattering seed for the hens. He pulled another sheet of birchbark from the pocket of his felt jacket, spun his charcoal stick in his fingers, and started again. His hand re-created her wavy, obsidian hair, curls straining against the confines of her braid, sometimes escaping across her upper back. Dark eyebrows, animated islands in the liquid light that cascaded over her pale, freckled skin. Blue-black eyes set wide across her visage, framed by smudges of cedar ash as was the fashion. Her lips, her lips, red and curved, the way Evangeline chewed on them whenever she concentrated, as she did now, tending her fowl. Gabriel bit his own lip to share the sensation. He studied her breasts, the smooth rounds of them, carefully concealed under her ocean-blue kirtle of felt, which was laced over a roughly woven linen-cloth shirt and extended into dual panels—tails, she called them—that billowed around her hips and over her lean, muscular legs, clad in deerskin to her ankles. Gabriel imagined the feel of her ankles, powerful and delicate at once, of her calves, her thighs. His breath caught as her kirtle-tails rolled and waved in the breeze, swaying like the ocean a thousand feet below the crest of this bec, the restless ocean that jovially tossed frothy waves skyward to catch the white-gold light of the afternoon sun as the unyielding and rambunctious tide turned back toward Glosekap Bay. The tide kept time in Cadia, and even so far above the water, Gabriel could hear the tide changing.

Gabriel knew he should go. He wasn't supposed to be here in the first place. He would see Evangeline later tonight for the signing of the contract, and then, after tomorrow, they would be together, always, forever, and his ever-tossed heart would be peaceful at last. But Gabriel had meager faith in tomorrow. Life had taught him well: Tomorrow doesn't exist until it arrives.

Evangeline turned toward Gabriel, looking down, not seeing him, eyes fixed on her task. At her heels scuttled Poc, the mutt, scattering dust and leaves, and growling to keep the lordly turkey away from the hen seed. She smiled at Poc and took his jaw in her hands. A wave of envy passed through Gabriel's stomach and wedged itself in his throat, and he forced his feet still to keep from rushing to her.

Gabriel lost his balance and, stepping back, snapped a twig under his moccasin. Evangeline spun around, squinting into the wood beyond the mossy stone walls surrounding her father's small farmyard and into the murmuring pines beyond. Gabriel froze, his ruddy green hunting tunic and brown skin fading into his sylvan hiding place, the living woods where the tips of the leaves were just starting to assume their rich autumn hues of scarlet and amber. The shadows were long now, orange and pink and gold as sunset approached, and though Gabriel was certain she'd seen him, Evangeline turned back to her charges, unalarmed.

"Eat, my girls," she said in a musical whisper. "Eat and lay. We'll need eggs for strength tomorrow. For strength and feasting." The chickens clucked in eloquent recognition of Evangeline's gentle command. Even they were devoted to her.

Just then, a voice called out, "Sunshine!" Gabriel recognized Benedict Bellefontaine's voice, coming from inside the house.

Gabriel studied the house and its hulking chimney. Except for the short summer season, life around Glosekap Bay was a constant struggle against cold, different kinds of cold, sometimes an ocean-wet whisper of coolness, sometimes a delicate sting of frost, sometimes a crackling seizure of ice. The fireplace was the largest and most important feature in every dwelling. Now in Second Summer, the days were warm again, but the nights grew ever longer. Gabriel smelled the afternoon and knew, or feared, that this winter would be as long and inclement as last year's. In generations past, the Ab'naki elders had taught the Cadians to read the fur of the foxes, and this season the fur was thick. Gabriel hoped the fireplace in the home he'd built for Evangeline would suffice in the cold, hungry winter ahead.

But today was not cold, it was warm, and the bec was bathed in golden vapors, the magical light of deep afternoon, and winter seemed distant. Gabriel's thoughts converged on tonight. Monsieur Bellefontaine had invited Basil and Gabriel to sign the documents of betrothal. It would be the first time he stepped into her home.

Gabriel closed his eyes and imagined what he'd see. He'd painted the picture in his mind innumerable times: a single room, protected from the offshore gales by boulders on the windward side, with two pine-shuttered windows facing away from the ocean, away from the northeasterly storms that blew across the bec in the coldest months, sparely furnished with a deep, comfortable ladder-back chair for Monsieur Bellefontaine and a bench and long table for Evangeline and their guests. A dirt floor, packed solidly, swept and decorated each morning with a new border pattern traced with a swirl of Evangeline's pointed broomstick.

Benedict Bellefontaine had lived seventy winters, which made Evangeline's father older than nearly all the men in the Cadian settlements around Glosekap Bay, and certainly older than Gabriel's father. Monsieur Bellefontaine's voice was indeed that of an old man, labored and graveled, and his brittle body bent heavily whenever he walked, which was less and less frequently as the seasons passed. He enjoyed the kindness of fellow Cadians from the village, Gabriel first among them, to help him with the planting and harvest, but he relied on Evangeline, his only family, to care for him and his home. And Evangeline loved her father fiercely. She kept the house, and him, as a mother keeps a cub. Gabriel knew she was torn at the thought of leaving her father alone. But Monsieur Bellefontaine had insisted that it was time.

14

He called out again. "Sunshine!"

"Coming, Father," Evangeline said softly. She gathered a basket of apples she'd picked up from the ground in the orchard that stretched from the back of the house into the meadow beyond. She draped her cornflower cloak over her arm. "Poc," she said. "Come. Let's press these apples into cider. Tomorrow we will marry our beloved Gabriel."

Evangeline stepped into the small log house, glancing back into the woods to where Gabriel stood unseen. "Tomorrow, everything becomes new," she said.

And—could it be? She smiled before pulling the Dutch door closed. Gabriel listened for the latch.

Tomorrow! Gabriel looked at the sky. The clouds over Glosekap Bay blushed golden pink, signifying imminent sunset. It was late. Soon twilight would descend. And there was much to do.

"I love you, my angel Evangeline," Gabriel whispered, but only the moss between the stones heard him. "I love you. No matter what happens."

He tucked his sketchbook into his foresleeve, securing it with a length of fabric, and turned into the woods.

eva

"Mr. Lejeune? Mr. Lejeune!" Mr. Denis doesn't yell, exactly, but his voice gets stern as he walks toward Gabe, who is still slouched over his notebook, still writing. "May we be so bold as to request your participation in today's recitation?" Mr. Denis always uses as many words as possible because he likes to remind anyone who's listening that he knows more words than they do. He obviously doesn't care that it's torture for everyone else.

It's not my fault I'm in a bad mood today. My father called me by my full name this morning. Evangeline. Da' is the only person in the world except Gabe who even knows my full name. Everyone else in Franktown calls me Eva. Everyone. Ada. Louise. Mr. Denis. Even Da', most of the time. Eva.

eva

That's it. Eva Bell. Done. Da' only calls me Evangeline one day a year, on my dead mother's birthday.

It's a whole routine. He wakes up early, puts a framed photograph of my mother on the kitchen table, and sits there and stares at it until I wake up and come downstairs. When I sit down at the table across from him, he says, still looking at the picture, "You are so beautiful, Evangeline." I don't know if he's talking to me or to my mother, because her name was Evangeline, too. Then he cries for the rest of the day. It happens every year.

Ada, who lives across the street, says that once men lose their wives, they add twenty years to their ages. Which I guess would put Da' north of seventy, in widower years. And Da's not just old in his mind, either, or in the way he behaves. It's his body, too. Da's got arthritis way worse even than Ada, who's over ninety and *should* have it. Some days he can barely make it out to his fields, or even just to the barn. "But we'll manage, Eva," he says. "We always do." I guess you have to be optimistic to be a farmer.

No one's ever really told me why my mother died the same day she gave birth to me. They just say vague things like "there were complications." They don't want me to think it was my fault that she died, that the complication was me. That my birth caused so much bleeding that she never regained consciousness. That Da' and my mother were definitely planning to name me Evangeline long before I was born, so that I don't get the idea that he named me Evangeline after she died because he really wanted his wife back, not a new daughter. This is why I never bring up my dead mother in conversation, because that kind of conversation always ends in a lie.

Gabe, who still hasn't looked up from his notebook, is the only other person I know whose mother is dead. I remember the first time he told me. I think we were seven, or maybe eight, and he was high up in a tree in the woods behind Ada's house. I yelled at him to come down, and he shushed me. "You're not my mother," he said, then pointed to a gnarled branch far out beyond the limb he was on. "Beehive."

"Be careful!" I yelled. "Come down!"

"Shh!" Gabe crawled across the branch like a panther, crouching low and moving slowly. A few bees buzzed around the branch, which was about as big around as Gabe was, which is to say not very big. Gabe kept moving, reaching out to grasp the branch with his hands, then pulling his body forward, each inch deliberate and intense. When he reached the hollowed-out knot that opened into the hive, he stopped. He flexed his fingers and took a deep breath. "Here goes." Slowly, deliberately, he maneuvered his hand down around the branch and reached into the hole. A few more bees buzzed around him, but Gabe's hand moved steadily, disappearing deeper into the opening. "Got it," he said.

Gabe pulled the honeycomb free from the hole and tossed it down to the mossy ground. He scooted back to the trunk of the tree and lowered himself down. "You're crazy," I said.

"It wouldn't hurt anyway, even if I got stung," he said, picking up the honeycomb and scooping honey onto his finger. "My mother is dead. Nothing hurts me anymore." He licked his finger and held out the honeycomb to me. "Have some."

Almost every day after that we went to the harbor at low tide. We left our shoes in the muck and climbed up under the dock. One day, Gabe found a quarter balanced on two of the beams, twenty feet above the seabed. He picked it up, breathed on it, shined it on his T-shirt, and handed it to me. "My life's savings," he said.

"Wow, a whole pack of gum," I said, but when I put it in my pocket I knew I wouldn't spend it.

We stayed there under the dock that day picking periwinkles off the posts and shivering in the midsummer chill and wondering if anyone noticed we were gone.

Gabe told me that he was probably going to run away one day. To disappear. I asked him why, but he just stared back at

19

me with clear, child eyes, blue and determined. I wanted to tell him that no matter where he wanted to run, ever, I would go with him, if he wanted me to. But I said nothing.

We stayed under the docks until the freezing tide licked at our backs and forced us out and up, choking water and gasping for air. Our shoes were gone. After I got home, and told Da' what happened to my shoes, he yelled at me. Didn't I know how dangerous the docks were? Didn't I remember how the Felician girl was washed away last year and turned up down in Nova Scotia? He told me that Gabe's father called to say he didn't want me hanging around with Gabe anymore. I said that was stupid, but Da' said it didn't matter. He said that when a rich man like Mr. Lejeune says he doesn't want his son hanging around with the daughter of a poor farmer like Da', he means it. And the sooner I got used to it, the sooner I would get over it. He said it all really matter-of-fact, like I wouldn't care, like Gabe wasn't my best and only friend.

That's pretty much the last time I talked to Gabe. He never really had any friends after that, just his notebook. He was always around, because everyone in Franktown goes to the same school, and I saw him every day, and I thought about him every night, but it was like part of him had disappeared and I didn't know how to find him.

Sometimes, I still pretend to talk to him. I pretend to reach out and take his troubled head in my hands.

"Mr. Lejeune!" Gabe doesn't look up from his writing. His pen speeds across the pages. "It is your turn to read, but it appears that you are otherwise occupied." Mr. Denis raps his hand on Gabe's desk. "Mr. Lejeune. May I inquire what it is that you are so feverishly documenting?" Mr. Denis daintily pulls Gabe's pen from his hand.

Gabe doesn't look up. He just puts his hand over his notebook, pressing it into the desk.

"Let us have a look!" In a tiny instant, Mr. Denis grabs the notebook from under Gabe's hand and whisks it violently upward, pages flying like a flapping chicken. Gabe grabs at it, clawing at the spiral binding, sending torn paper floating into the air like feathers, but Mr. Denis holds the notebook up out of his reach and quickly steps away. "Please, share this masterpiece. Surely your words have more literary merit than this laborious Longfellow we are wasting our time on."

Gabe's lanky body freezes, stiff in his chair, eyes fixed on the floor, hair flopping back over his face. He is awkwardly good-looking, olive-skinned with clear, green-blue eyes, but you have to look pretty hard to see it. His clothes are always rumpled, his sneakers worn, and he never has a coat warm enough for the weather.

John Baptiste, all blond and square-jawed and varsity-jacketed, snickers and winds his finger around his ear, making the crazy symbol, but I pretend not to see. Gabe is not crazy. He is strange, but he is not crazy. I know that much.

"Would you like to read aloud?" Mr. Denis says. "No? Then allow me to give voice to your words." Mr. Denis walks to the front of the room and clears his throat. "Ladies and gentlemen, an original work by Gabe Lejeune, Esquire."

I watch Gabe. He is staring at me. It's the first time I've seen his eyes straight on since that day under the docks, and even though they seem darker now, they are still full of determination, and they pierce into mine and I know he remembers, too. I stare back.

I know him.

He knows me.

"Evangeline," says Mr. Denis, reading from the notebook. My stomach drops suddenly. What did he just say?

"Evangeline," he repeats.

No. I bow my head. I get that strange kind of nausea that comes in a wave over your body and brain right after you cut yourself, that kind of sinking sickness that tells you the worst is yet to come. I pull the hood of my sweatshirt around and across my mouth. My heartbeat gets deeper, stronger, and thumps in my ear.

"Evangeline," says Mr. Denis again, his eyes scanning the page. "Evangeline, Evangeline, Evangeline, Evangeline." Mr. Denis turns the page. "Evangeline. Evangeline."

He flips a few more pages. "Evangeline." He stops. "Well, Mr. Lejeune, it seems as if you are not as far off-topic as I feared. You've got the right poet, just the wrong poem. We are not reading 'Evangeline,' also by Longfellow, in this class. Instead, we are muddling through 'The Courtship of Miles Standish,' and it is your turn to contribute to the recitation. Please take it from 'Over his countenance flitted a shadow . . .'" He drops the notebook back on Gabe's desk. Gabe slams his hand over it.

I am frozen.

"Freak," Louise whispers. John Baptiste snickers and shakes his head. I hide behind my hair, thanking God I have hair to hide behind. I peek out into the classroom and realize that not everyone is looking at me. Of course. No one knows that Evangeline is my full name. No one knows that Gabe is sitting over there writing *my* name over and over.

"'The Courtship of Miles Standish,' Mr. Lejeune," Mr. Denis says. "Please begin."

But Gabe does not begin. He slowly stands up, then stuffs

his notebook into his backpack, bunches his windbreaker in his fist, walks straight over to my desk, and says, "I'm sorry."

Then Gabe turns toward the door and pushes his way into the hall and leaves.

"Good-bye, Mr. Lejeune," Mr. Denis says.

I slip my hand into my jacket pocket and take Gabe's quarter in my fingers.

Gabriel

GABRIEL STRUCK HIS HEELS AGAINST HIS MARE, Eulalie, who responded with a brusque trot across the rippled, mucky flats of the darse. She moved with staccato steps between the groves of Irish moss and clusters of moules, between the tiny pools of abandoned seawater glistening golden with the reflected light of the falling sun. At high tide, this stretch would lie beneath thirty feet of water, but at low tide the exposed seabed stretched far out into Glosekap Bay, linking the mainland becs and marshes to the islands. Dories and whaleboats, temporarily landed until the water's return, sat like stranded toys in the muck.

The Glosekap tides were ferocious, fast, more like an insistent, unstoppable wave than a slow rise, plunging some thirty feet of water from Glosekap Bay into the darse, the narrow harbor where the Manan River emptied into the sea. Twice a day the wave rolled into the darse, sometimes angrily, sometimes merely resolute, speedily transforming the landscape into a seascape, before retreating with equal haste. Only the secrets passed through generations allowed the Cadian fishermen to navigate it, so complex were its currents. Many of the oldest stories told around Cadian fireplaces were of those unlucky enough to be carried off into the desolate heart of the ocean. Bodies were rarely found.

Twice in their history had an angry, storm-fed tide washed through their village, destroying it.

Now, some forty summers after the last flooding, an elaborate system of dikes protected the basin where Pré-du-sel was built. All Cadians, male and female, worked on the dikes as soon as they were big enough to move earth. The tide was unrelenting, and the erosion of the dikes was constant. Repairs were always needed.

Basil Lajeunesse, Gabriel's father and the village blacksmith, often spoke of the three New Colony ships that once anchored in Glosekap Bay, back when Gabriel was a very small boy. They shone, he said, glinting like ice even in the summer.

As soon as the ships were spotted, the villagers extinguished their fires so that no telltale column of smoke would incite the ships to attack the town or the dikes. But the foreign ships never released a dory, no person ever landed, no contact was made, not a single shot was fired, and most important, not a dike was compromised.

The presence of the ships nonetheless took a great toll on the village. It was autumn when they came and the days were still temperate, but by the time they left some five weeks later, the first snows were falling. The harvest, already thin that year, went unharvested. With no fires burning and precious little food to eat, thirty-four villagers died.

27

Among the dead was Gabriel's mother, who drew her last breath on the day the ships disappeared, as Basil cradled their stillborn son in his arms.

Basil never recovered.

Fifteen years later, men in the village still argued about the ships. Some believed the village was never in danger in the first place, never even spotted. Some said the ships simply sank. Some claimed there were never any ships at all. Basil the blacksmith, whose vocation ranked him as the most powerful man in Pré-du-sel, believed that the sailors were unable to decipher the tides well enough to land there and simply sailed away, taking word of the harbor's inaccessibility to the New Colonies. He predicted that the Glosekap tides would continue to protect this remote Cadian village, and that never again would the ships return.

But if they did, he said, all Cadians would be compelled to resist. In the name of the dead.

eva

L ouise is talking.

"I mean, if it was Gabe's brother, the whole thing could have been sexy. Paul is definitely the hotter of *les frères Lejeune*." We step out of the front door and into the foggy street. "But Gabe? *Je ne sais pas*, Eva. He's just weird. He's always been weird."

"Not always," I say.

When he looked at me today, it was like I knew him again. His eyes were familiar, and I remembered their deep-sea light, luminescent like the lantern fish that rise to the surface of the ocean at night.

What did he mean when he said he was sorry?

"Speaking of Paul, have you heard?" Louise is still talking.

"Hm?" I'm distracted.

"I'm not really supposed to tell anyone about this, but my dad says he was taken to the hospital in Bangor last night. He has to stay there for a couple of days for all these tests. Of course, being the town meathead, all Dad is worried about is that the Franktown High Mariners will lose their top scorer for the season. But supposedly it's *sérieux*. Cancer maybe."

"So what?" I say. As soon as I say it, I hear it, and I know it sounds wrong. I meant so what about the hockey team, not so what about Paul.

"Wow, harsh," Louise says. "He could die, Eva."

"I didn't mean it like that," I say. "I meant—" I stall again, and say, "That's awful."

Suddenly Gabe materializes out of the fog. I don't even see him until I practically bump into him. It's that foggy. Thick, gooey fog that forms droplets on your face if you walk too fast through it. A real pea-souper, Ada would call it, so thick you can feel it in your mouth.

"Oops," I say to Gabe. "Didn't see you."

He doesn't answer. He just stares at me. He blinks, and little wisps of fog waft across his eyelids like clouds across a landscape.

"How is your brother?" Louise says to Gabe.

Gabe smiles stiffly at Louise and nods his head, then

30

reaches out and grabs my arm. "Come with me. I want to show you something," he says. "OK?"

"She's busy," Louise says, carefully prying his fingers from my arm. "Tell Paul we said hi. Come on, Eva." Louise grabs the cuff of my oversized fisherman's sweater, the one that I wear almost every single day, the one that used to be Da's until he got a new one and gave it to me, but only because I asked for it, like, seventy-five times. She quickens her pace, pulling me along like a toddler tripping behind an impatient babysitter. "Eva, we have to go," she says commandingly.

Gabe starts trotting along with us, just a step behind me and gaining. "Please," he says. "Come."

"Hey, Eva!" comes another voice from the fog. "Eva!"

It's John Baptiste. He could be ten feet away or a hundred yards, I can't tell. I don't answer him, I just keep shuffling along with Louise, with Gabe at my heels.

Gabe walks faster. "Please," he says. Then he whispers, so only I can hear it and not Louise. "Evangeline."

Then he stops cold. Louise and I take three more steps, far enough so that when I shake my sleeve free of Louise's grasp and turn around, nearly all of Gabe is obscured by the fog, except for his outstretched hand, smooth and lithe and steady and strong, probably from all that writing. It's beautiful.

"It's OK, Louise," I say, leaning toward the hand. "I'll see you later."

Louise shakes her head, muttering something I can't hear, and steps away, into the fog. I turn around to watch her sneakers disappear. *"Au revoir,"* she says as she slips out of sight.

I step forward, toward Gabe's hand. "So," I say, stopping after one step. "What do you want to show me?"

Gabe doesn't answer. He takes my wrist in his fingers and starts walking, pulling me along behind him.

"Are you OK?" I say.

No answer.

"Let go," I say. "I can walk." But Gabe just grips my hand tighter, slicing a path through the fog just wide enough for us both. "Where are we going?"

"Harbor," he says.

When it's this foggy, most people walk along slowly, looking down at the ground to make sure they don't trip or step in dog crap or something. But Gabe is moving fast. I'm practically double-stepping to keep up with him. "I haven't been to the harbor with you since—" I stop.

"That was a long time ago," Gabe says, and starts walking faster.

We walk all the way through the four blocks of "downtown" Franktown and out onto the single dock that juts into Franktown Harbor.

I know when we reach the dock only because I hear the Manan River, which is really more like a stream, trickling into the harbor from its outlet just a few yards away. I feel the slats of the dock creaking beneath our footsteps—his strong and certain, mine shuffling and wary. But I can't see the end of the dock, or how high the water is.

"Down or up," he says, and I know he's asking whether I want to climb down and straddle one of the crossbeams under the dock like we used to do before everything changed, or stay on top of the dock, where things are safer. I say, "Up."

"Up," Gabe repeats, and I can hear his disappointment and already I wish I'd chosen "down."

We feel for the edge of the dock with our feet and sit at the very tip. Gabe sheds his Converse sneakers and dangles his feet over the edge. "Take your shoes off," he says. I do, and I dangle my feet over the edge, too, right next to Gabe's.

I try to forget that I don't know him anymore. I pretend not to wonder what he's thinking. Instead I wonder about how far away the water is from my feet. Not that it matters, because the tide changes fast. Wherever it is now isn't where it will be next time I check.

"I know what today is," Gabe says. "I know what it means." He's talking about my mother.

And now I know that no one else but Gabe understands me, no one else in the whole town, no matter how much they want to, not my father, not Ada, not Louise. No one. Only Gabe. My motherless best friend.

Gabe puts his arm around my neck and locks his strong hands across my chest, drawing my head to his shoulder and my arm to his lap. His grip is not sad like Da's, not clumsy. Gabe holds me tighter than that. I can hear, or maybe feel, the deep, slow thumping of his heart. I close my eyes and breathe, feeling the sea mist coat my lungs with salt air.

He sweeps my hair away from my eyes with his strong fingers and buries his eyes into mine. "Cry, Evangeline," he says. "Cry today."

And I do. I cry.

I cry, hard at first, then softer with short, baby-girl sobs, Gabe's hand resting on my cheek. I have always imagined what it would feel like to cry and not have to explain why. Now I know. It feels like home.

When I am finished crying, I wipe my eyes and realize that the fog has begun to thin. It is still day, and I can see the harbor dories, bright yellow and blue and red, bobbing in the gray-green waves. It is nearing high tide. One dory, a white one, catches a flash of sun and reflects it back to us, illuminating Gabe's face like a spotlight. I see from the tear tracks that he has been crying, too, even though he never made a sound. He held me against his steady heart, and cried with me, never shaking, never shifting, moving only to breathe.

"You know, you're going to flunk Mr. Denis's class if you don't start paying attention to those old stories he makes us read," I say, sniffling and pretending to laugh.

"I don't care," he says, stroking my hair and looking out to sea. "I don't like the old stories anyway. They don't have anything to do with us. I'd rather write my own."

Gabriel

EULALIE'S CANTER WAS SHARP, JARRING GABRIEL'S spine, and he wished he'd taken the time to strap on her saddle when he'd left home that morning instead of taking her out bareback. He clicked his tongue and she slowed to a walk.

Gabriel untied his moccasins and lashed them to Eulalie's bridle, then jumped down into the muck. It was cold, bracingly so, but he relished the feeling of the wet sea mud on his feet.

Within steps his soles went pins-and-needles numb, the same way they had so many years ago when he, like all the village children, was sent down at low tide to dig for clams during the harvest weeks. Whoever dug up the most clams got to keep his entire sackful. The rest were divided equally among the village households. When the time came to tally, Gabriel always had the most clams, except when he secretly filled Evangeline's sack to make certain she would win. He did this even though his angry father would punish him every time he fell short, sending him back into the harbor, sometimes after dark, sometimes in the path of the tide, to bring up more clams. Gabriel's feet froze on those nights. Once, when Gabriel returned home with a full bucket, his bare feet were stiff, ice-blue in the candlelight. "My son," cried Monsieur Lajeunesse, and he rubbed prickly warmth back into them. "My son, forgive me," he pleaded. "I have pushed you too hard." But Gabriel wasn't listening to his father's apology. He was thinking only of Evangeline, and how she'd have plenty of clams to share with her father that night. The next week, when Gabriel again returned home after moonrise with a bucket of clams and bloodless, frozen feet, Monsieur Lajeunesse did not rub them. His father said coldly, "Only after you have cleaned the clams may you sit by the fire." That night, Gabriel's feet froze deeply, and it was many days before he walked again.

37

Gabriel tugged at Eulalie's reins, nudging her toward the dock. The tide was on its way back now, and they didn't have much time.

A sudden glint of light from beyond piney St. Isabel Island pierced his eyes. Gabriel started and stared. The light was gone as quickly as it had flashed, and Gabriel saw nothing. He frowned. The sun was too low to strike a wave with such brightness, such precision. Gabriel squinted out to sea. Could it have been a glint from one of the temporary low-tide pools? A reflection off the pink granite rocks at the base of St. Isabel? Gabriel's mind raced for an explanation.

Another glint, even sharper this time. No. This was no pool-glisten, no rock. This glint was needlelike, precise, not accidental, and it was aimed directly at the darse.

Another flash.

A ship? It couldn't be. There were no ships in Glosekap Bay. He patted Eulalie, who snorted at the oncoming tide. Gabriel shushed her and focused his gaze. Eulalie shook her neck. Another glint. And another. The source of the light was moving, slowly, across Glosekap.

So it was a ship. It had to be. Gabriel drew a breath and held it. A ship. Just outside the darse.

Heaven, not now.

Gabriel's heart sped and his eyes darted back and forth across the bay. Ships were mythic, nearly unknown in Cadia, as none of the Cadian settlements had the money or power to build them. Gabriel's world was all dories and whaleboats and sometimes, when the alewives ran, Ab'naki canoes from the east. Unthreatening boats. Not weapons. Not ships.

Gabriel rubbed his eyes. Perhaps it was an illusion, perhaps a monster. Please, anything but a ship. He tensed his jaw and squinted, setting off a quiet rumble in his temple. Please, do not let this be the day Basil foretold.

Another glint emerged from behind St. Isabel. Then two at once. Two ships? It couldn't be. No.

Eulalie snorted. "Quiet," Gabriel scolded.

Another glint. And another. Soon there were four glints of light, flashing simultaneously in the harbor.

Mesmerized, terrified, Gabriel felt his eyes glaze over and stomach sink in realization: After so many years, the New Colony ships had returned.

"No!" he shouted. His heartbeat grew loud in his ear. Fast, driving, pounding rhythms.

The frigid water lapped at the cold muck just ahead of Gabriel's feet, but Gabriel was flushed, sweating, desperate to banish this vision, and did not move. This could not be. Not before tomorrow. No. Gabriel forced breath back into his lungs, slowly. Eulalie snorted again.

Gabriel silenced her and turned his gaze to the becs, to the highlands above the bay. There, rising over the ocean's rocky caverns, was Evangeline's bec, and above it, a column of smoke from her chimney. Any other day it would have warmed Gabriel to see the sight. But not today. He looked back at the ships, then up at the bec, then back to the ships, to and fro in speechless panic. Could they see the smoke, too?

Gabriel had to tell his father. He needed Basil, or someone, to see the ships, to make this real, or banish it from his mind.

"Come, Eulalie," Gabriel said sternly, leaping onto the mare and pointing her toward the river's mouth. "Run, Eulalie. Run," he whispered.

Hearts leaping, they sped together, past the harbor, over the hill and into the fruitful valley, where the village of Pré-du-sel huddled, blissfully glowing under the alabaster steeple of the church and the towering chimney of Basil Lajeunesse's village smithy, unaware of the predators at the head of the tide-swept darse.

eva

It's been forever since I've seen you," Louise says from behind her sunglasses. She picks at her black nail polish. I realize that I've never seen Louise with fresh nail polish. She must start picking at it as soon as it dries. *"Qu'est-ce qui se passe?"*

"Shut up," I say. "I see you every day."

I lean against the slow, misty breeze oozing up Commercial Street from the sea. It was sunny today, mostly. Indian summer, everyone calls it, but Mr. Denis says we're supposed to call it Second Summer to be culturally sensitive. Ada still calls it Summer of All Saints, which I guess is what the old-timers say.

"The sun feels good," I say. "It hasn't been sunny for a month."

"Franktown sucks," says Louise, pointing at a weathered row of town houses. *"Regardes."*

Louise is right. The sun is a mixed blessing around here. It just shows all of Franktown's cracks. There isn't a building around, house or store or gas station or barn, without peeling paint and weeds. Half the houses are for sale. The biggest thing in town is a propane tower with our zip code painted on it: 04647.

"Anyway, you know what I mean," Louise says. "You've, like, disappeared. What's your story?"

I don't answer, even though I know what she wants to hear about. I've been pretty quiet the last few days. I've got a lot on my mind, I guess.

"Fine, I'll do the talking," says Louise. "I don't get the Gabe thing. All he does is mope around and scribble in that stupid notebook. And why can't he get a haircut? His father is the richest man in Washington County."

"I don't know what you're talking about," I say. Rough translation: Drop it.

"I just don't get the appeal," Louise says. "I mean, he's so, I don't know, *morose*. What's he got to be so mopey about? I don't even see how he's related to the rest of his family." She picks off another chunk of polish. "He should take grooming lessons from his brother. Personality lessons, *aussi*."

"Gabe's not Paul," I say.

"No kidding," Louise says. "You could do so much better, Eva. John Baptiste has been all over you for months. And he is looking *très* hot lately."

I roll my eyes. Louise can't fathom how anyone could ever resist the gorgeous, wealthy John Baptiste. He's supposedly Franktown's most desirable catch. Which is exactly why I don't like him.

"And he has a nice car," she says. "And he doesn't carry a stupid notebook around everywhere he goes."

"That's because he doesn't know how to write," I say.

"Seriously, Eva," Louise says. "Do you really like this guy? Because this is going to take some getting used to."

I don't know how to answer without making her upset, and I really don't want to talk about it, because Louise wouldn't get it anyway—that Gabe understands me, sees me, that ever since my mother's birthday, all I've thought about is the way his deep breaths and slow heartbeat sounded against my ears while I cried on the docks against his shoulder. I just say: "He's different."

"Understatement," Louise says. She goes back to picking her nails.

"I'll see you," I say. "Let's hang out, maybe this weekend?"

"Wait, don't tell me. You're blowing me off again," Louise says, or more like scoffs. *"Quel choc."* She pulls the hoodstrings of her sweatshirt straight down with a jerk and disappears into the hood. She heads up the hill toward the tiny Franktown library, where we used to go every day after school, supposedly to do homework but really to read magazines. "Hey, by the way, did Gabe tell you about Paul?"

"What about Paul?" I say.

"My father says Paul needs a bone marrow transplant. They're looking for a donor."

"I didn't—"

"I thought Gabe would have talked to you about it. Brothers usually make good donors."

I don't say anything. Gabe hasn't said a word about his brother to me. I've been wondering, but I haven't asked.

"Anyway, bye," Louise says. She turns and steps away.

"Bye," I say. I watch her walk up the hill for a few minutes. And then I turn toward the harbor and walk toward the dock, where Gabe has promised to meet me.

44

Gabriel

THE POWERFUL ARMS OF BASIL THE BLACKSMITH rippled as he grasped the hammer with heavy, elbow-length leather gloves and slammed it onto the anvil with a tremendous *clang*.

"Do you hear me?" he said. "I don't believe you." *Clang*. Basil wore a black leather apron that glimmered in the glow of the fire under the great iron-and-cedar forge that sat in the center of the dirt floor. The forge lorded over the ember-lit shop, its radiant heat causing sweat to drain from Basil's brow. Shadows cast in four directions took the shapes of anvils, clamps, rods, and Basil's broad shoulders.

"But Father, I saw," Gabriel protested from the doorway. "Four ships. I have no doubt."

"Quiet!" Basil shouted. "There are no ships. You are wrong." Basil slammed the hammer down again with a terrible *clank* that Gabriel felt in his teeth. "You're supposed to be working out on the dikes, searching for breaches and protecting your village. The tide is unrelenting, Gabriel, and the threats, the real threats, are many."

Gabriel muttered a curse.

"Father—"

"Enough!" Basil held up the horseshoe with his tongs, twisting it back and forth in the air to inspect it. "There. Another perfect shoe. Gabriel, bring the horse around to the . . ." He waved a gloved finger toward the back entrance.

46

Gabriel, silenced, walked toward the large doors on the back wall, past the boy operating the shoulder-high bellows used to fan the hell-hot fire that Basil had kept alive for four years running, burning coal harvested from the marshes. The fire was hot enough to melt metal, and the marbled, pocked skin that covered Basil's forearms and neck proved it was hot enough to melt flesh, too. The boy, drenched and sinewy, looked up at Gabriel through dusty, tired eyes, slowing the bellows for a moment.

"Attend!" Basil shouted at the boy. "Fire!"

"Monsieur," said the boy. He inhaled deeply, rose to his toes, and extended the bellows-handle over his head, then thrust downward to the floor, sending oxygen-rich air into the forge to feed the devilish heat.

Gabriel pushed open the back door. There were two horses in the courtyard, Eulalie and one of Notary Leblanc's massive workhorses, Nog. He was a tall horse with colossal feet, bred to work in the hayfields. His back was speckled black and gray with a shorn mane and cropped tail. He whinnied and shook his massive head with a sputter. Gabriel grasped Nog's rein and led him lumbering into the shop, where Basil stood with a freshly shaped shoe. Gabriel stroked Nog's nose while Basil raised his back leg and held the shoe against his hoof. "Perfect," he said, drawing a nail from the pocket of his apron.

47

"At least someone here knows what he's doing," came the voice from the doorway. There stood Jean-Baptiste Leblanc, the notary's son, tall and expensively dressed, the glowing forge lengthening his cheekbones and his shadow. Jean-Baptiste was still unmarried, despite his good looks and his family's wealth. With a dozen horses in their employ, the Leblancs were Basil's best customers.

"Master Leblanc," said Basil. "Welcome." He motioned to a bench at the side of the shop, a motion that Jean-Baptiste ignored.

Gabriel was wary of Jean-Baptiste. He knew that Jean-Baptiste, like every man in Pré-du-sel, desired Evangeline.

Even now, just hours before their wedding, Gabriel knew that Jean-Baptiste coveted Evangeline, and he fixed his eyes on his rival. Tomorrow, he told himself. *Tomorrow she will be mine, and there will be no more threats from him, or anyone.*

"I'm sorry, Monsieur Lajeunesse," said Jean-Baptiste, indulgently enunciating each sound in Basil's name. "I'm afraid I have been eavesdropping unintentionally. Did I hear something about ships? My apologies, but what nonsense is this?"

"Just nonsense, as you say," said Basil. "There are no ships. Today is not the day."

48

Jean-Baptiste pulled his head back and squinted at Gabriel. "I see," he said. He turned back to Basil.

Basil wiped his brow with his scarred forearm. "Come, Gabriel. Hold Nog's bridle and steady him. We must shoe this horse for young Leblanc."

eva

We've been driving up Boot Cove Road for fifteen minutes now, or maybe more, and we're not really driving anyway, it's more like speeding, heading east, listening to an old Led Zeppelin song. Gabe wants to get to Quoddy Head before sunset so we can watch the stars come up over Passamaquoddy Bay, even if it means doubling the speed limit the whole way.

"I've never seen a cop out here," he says.

Gabe's car isn't fancy, just a secondhand sedan with a bench seat and electric windows. The baby-blue hood doesn't match the rest of the body, which is chocolate brown.

Gabe looks different today, grown-up and serious, hair pushed back from his broad forehead, light whiskers sprouting from his angled jawline. His eyes smile in unison with the corners of his mouth as he hits the gas again. Yesterday he qualified as cute. Today he's handsome.

"I like your car," I say, thinking how stupid I sound when I do. I look at his hands, clasped together with fingers locked, dangling over the top of the steering wheel. He drives with his wrists.

"It'll be all right once I get the hood painted," Gabe says. "I bought it last week from the want ads on the back page of the *Lubec Lighthouse*." He pats the wheel and smiles, a sideways smile. "It's a birthday present for myself." He speeds up even more.

"You gave yourself a birthday present?" I ask. "Who does that?" I'm trying to flirt, but just as I smile we hit a pothole and he turns to look at the road and doesn't see.

"I do," he says, swerving into the oncoming lane to avoid a shredded tire on the roadside. "I always have. Every year."

"OK," I say. I want to say "That's weird," but I don't, because he probably won't think that's flirting. Instead, I say, "Well, you made a great choice." I roll down my window. "What else did you get for your birthday?"

Gabriel looks over at me, his blue eyes tender, hazy. He scrunches his brow and shakes his head. "Just this."

"Come on," I say. "Nothing else?"

Gabe shakes his head. I see his notebook on the dashboard, sliding back and forth as the road winds toward Quoddy. I watch it, hoping it slides off the dashboard and onto the seat, splitting open for just a moment so I can glimpse inside. "What about your brother?" I ask.

"He got a Mercedes," he says.

"What?"

"My brother. For his last birthday. He got a Mercedes."

I'm angry at whoever gave Paul a birthday Mercedes and gave Gabe nothing. Which, I'm guessing, would be their father, Mr. Basil Lejeune, Esq., the only lawyer in Franktown. He considers Paul, the big hockey star, his family's only real success story, after himself, of course. Quiet, scribbling, second son Gabe doesn't deserve a Mercedes. "No, I mean how is he doing?"

"What?"

"Louise told me he was sick or something. Is he going to be—"

I can't even finish my question before Gabe turns up the Led Zeppelin song on the radio. Loud. "Many times I've lied . . . ," he sings. He rolls down his window and speeds up, the wind blowing his mop of hair back into his face, plastering it against his cheek. He disappears behind it. "Many times I've wondered . . ."

I just sit and look out the window at the ocean appearing and disappearing through the pine trees in flashes of infinity.

Quoddy Head appears in the distance. Gabe takes hold of the steering wheel with his left hand and slides his right hand over on top of mine. He feels warm on my skin. I turn my hand over and grasp his.

Gabe doesn't talk to me, and somehow it's OK. I don't want this drive to end.

Gabriel

BASIL AND GABRIEL, IN MATCHING WAISTCOATS of navy broadcloth fastened with bone buttons, ascended the bec in a loose fog that floated between the star points like gossamer, like the antique shawl of lace and linen that would flow softly from Evangeline's head and drape over her breast tomorrow, like the skirt of ancient silk that would whirl around her as they danced in the orchard.

"I see no ships," said Basil the blacksmith with a breath of relief and a scoff of superior bemusement. "In a lively fog such as this, light from the ships would find shore. I see none."

Gabriel had seen the ships. He knew they were there. But because he'd rather not have seen them, because his world was only complicated by them, because more imperative than his need to be heard was his need to be married tomorrow, Gabriel lied, "I must have been mistaken, Father. You are right. There are no ships."

Basil and Gabriel dismounted and tied up the horses at Evangeline's wall. They approached the door and Basil raised his hand to knock. "No ships."

"Ah, but there are," said Benedict, who opened the door before Basil's hand made contact. He stood, bent, at the doorway. "I have seen them. Welcome, welcome." He stooped to bow to his guests, soon to be relatives. He teetered, just catching his balance with one hand on the doorframe and the other pressed onto his cane. "Evangeline!" he called faintly, his voice scratched and wearied by seventy winters. "Our friends are here." He smiled. "Our family, I mean."

"Ships?" Basil repeated. "Are you certain, Benedict?"

"Yes, old friend," Benedict replied. "My angel has shown them to me. Four ships, or perhaps more. Evangeline!" he called again wearily. "But they are friends, these ships, I am certain of it, as certain as I am that you, young Gabriel, and you, Monsieur Basil, are friends of ours."

Benedict moved feebly aside, revealing the warm light of the house behind him.

"If there are ships, they mean ill," Basil uttered. "I surmise

54

evil. Benedict, please. Show me these ships." Basil pushed Gabriel aside and took the old man by the arm. "Come. Show me." He guided Benedict onto the doorstep.

Together, as quickly as old Benedict could move, the pair of widowers stepped out onto the stony path that led to the edge of the bec, arms locked. "We are in no danger," Benedict said cheerfully. "Perhaps they intend to trade."

"Show me the ships," was Basil's grim response.

"Perhaps the crops have failed in the New Colonies," Benedict offered. "Perhaps they are here for help." He continued to gesture as the old friends walked on out of Gabriel's earshot.

Gabriel turned back to the doorway. There, with the fiery light flickering behind her, stood Evangeline. His eyes softened at the sight of hers, blue and black and green together, so deep and dark and yet so filled with light. He wanted to enter those eyes, to gain access to her very soul through them.

She smiled. "Gabriel."

His greeting never reached his lips, so entrancing it was to hear her say his name. "Come," she said next. "Let us walk with our fathers." She started up the path.

Gabriel followed Evangeline, who followed Basil and Benedict up the rocky path to the top of the bec and the star-speckled sky beyond. He watched her legs bend and sway as she negotiated the rocks in her soft moccasins. Gabriel adored her.

Benedict and Basil shuffled to the edge of the bec. "We should be able to see them from here," Benedict wheezed. He waved a finger toward the bay. "Somewhere."

"There," Basil said grimly, pointing at a grouping of lights flickering in the bay. "There." He stood, legs planted territorially onto the ground, arms held out from his sides, defiant and statuesque. But even from his position ten paces away, Gabriel could see Basil's hands tremble.

"New Colonies," Gabriel whispered to Evangeline as they approached their fathers.

"By God, it is they," Basil said, his voice low but strong, audible above the wind on the swirling bec grass. "We will fight them. They will not take us. They will not take our people. They will not take this land."

"Basil, old friend," Benedict said, taking the blacksmith's elbow. "Surely they are not here to attack us. We have nothing they want in our simple village. The New Colonies are the richest in the world, and they have no need for us. They must mean well. They did not kill the last time they were here."

"They did not kill?" Basil snapped. "Have you forgotten

those starved into death? They killed my wife! My second son! As sure as if they shot them."

Gabriel stepped forward. "Father."

"We will fight them," Basil said. He turned away from the ships and stared back at Gabriel. "We will fight them, Gabriel. By the memory of your mother, and your brother, we will resist."

All stood in silence for a moment.

"Basil," said Benedict, piercing the wind with a pleading voice. "Please, reconsider. Let us not greet these outsiders with aggression. Perhaps they mean no harm at all. Let us welcome them." He paused to catch a breath. "Whatever is to come, we are safer unarmed."

Basil exploded. "Naive!" he shouted. "Would you give away our homes? Our names?" He strode down the path toward the house. "Gabriel!" he shouted.

"Basil, old friend," said Benedict, struggling to keep up. "Stay and have some cider. Perhaps you are right." He turned and winked at Evangeline. "Basil!"

Basil stopped abruptly without turning around. Benedict caught up to him, took his arm, and together they walked back to the house, arm in arm again, Basil growling curses against the tyranny of the New Colonies.

Gabriel turned to Evangeline, then back out to the bay.

He felt her hand slip into his. It was a comfortable fit, her skin warm and soft between the calluses, his pulsing with blood. He closed his eyes, squinting behind his eyelids to force a picture of forever, of her and him. His temples throbbed with love.

"You are my greatest friend," Evangeline said to Gabriel. "And tomorrow you will be my husband." Evangeline took his hand and brought it to her cheek, letting his thumb brush her lip, where he felt the humidity of her sigh, understanding through his fingertips that this being, this unbearably beautiful being, trusted him. "Oh, Gabriel. Whatever happens, promise that we will be together. Forever."

"My beloved," he whispered.

eva

I don't know why I am surprised when Gabe tries to kiss me. But he does, full on the lips, when he drops me off in front of my house, and I *am* surprised.

We spent two hours out at Quoddy Head watching the stars slowly fade in to fill the sky over the sea. In the height of summer the place is usually crawling with Canadian tourists, but tonight ours was the only car in the parking lot. Gabe leaned against a rock on a protected ledge out near the candy-striped lighthouse, and I leaned against Gabe.

"Starry, starry night," he whispered. "Paint your palette blue and gray . . ."

"What?"

"It's a song," he said, "about a man no one understood." And then he started singing, quietly, in my ear.

"No one ever sang to me before," I said when he finished. Then, under my breath, so quietly that I don't think he heard me, I said, "Thank you."

He clasped his hands over mine and told me I couldn't get up until I'd counted all the stars.

"That would take forever," I said.

"Perfect," he said, tightening his grasp.

Now, back at my house, Gabe parks right outside the living room window, and it makes me self-conscious, and I start wondering if Da' can see, and I wonder if Da' would recognize Gabe, and whether he'd remember banning Gabe from my life so many years ago.

Gabe swings the lever into park and turns toward me. He reaches around to put his hand on my far shoulder and leans his face toward mine, smiling faintly. I look up into his eyes, those clear eyes that I know so well, and at that moment the Gabe I've just fallen in love with gets all mixed up with the Gabe who scribbled incessantly in that notebook of his, the Gabe I watched as a child crawl out onto a branch no bigger than he was to pull honeycomb from a hive, the Gabe who gave me his life's savings under the docks that day, the day we hid together, away from the world, and pretended not to care that neither of us had a mother to worry, to wonder where we were, to be glad when we came home safe.

And all of a sudden there's just too much in his eyes and too much in my head and I freak out and pull away from him.

And he pulls away from me.

"I'm sorry," I say. "It's just—"

"No," he says. "I—" He looks down at the steering wheel. He whispers. "I'm sorry."

And I look over and see shame in his face, and also anger and fear and loneliness, and I want to fix them all, and I want him to fix me, too, and before he can say anything else I lean over and take his face in my hands and I press my lips against his and hold them there, intently, for I don't know how long. My eyes are closed, but then I open them and realize that he is staring back at me, eyes wide in shock.

I pull away again, already regretting the gamble gone bad. But he catches the back of my head with his hand. Holding my head steady, Gabe pulls us together and finally, after the third try, we connect. His lips crash into mine, desperate and intent and as strong as his hands, and mine push back, more intent even than his, and we press together, and his lips become my lips, and his breath is my breath, and I don't care where our noses are or whether I'm using too much tongue or even where his hands are. All I know is that I've never felt anything better in my life.

It takes over everything in me, and I wonder if I've ever felt anything at all before.

What I've wanted so badly that I couldn't say it out loud was to be connected to Gabe. And in this moment, I am. I feel alive. Not happy, really, because there is so much sadness in him, in his eyes, his voice, his lips. But he is so alive, and I am so alive.

"Home," I say, when our lips finally separate.

"What?"

"Nothing."

The light flickers on outside my front door. Da' has seen us.

"I better go," I struggle to say.

I climb out the passenger door, closing it weakly behind me just as Gabe says, "Wait!" He pops his door and leaps over the corner of the car, intercepting me in the headlights. He smiles, wrinkling his brow like a hound puppy and holding up his index finger. "One more kiss?"

"But my da'," I say.

"One more."

I laugh, and he strides slowly toward me, grabbing the belt loops on each of my hips and yanking me, gently, into his embrace, warm and secure and welcoming. The embrace becomes another kiss. And I'm alive again for another moment.

"Good night," he says. He cups my chin in his hand and fills my eyes with his distant ocean-blues. "Evangeline." He gets back in the car and rolls down his window. "My angel," he says as he drives slowly away.

I wave at the house so Da' can see me, in case he is watching, which he probably is. Then I head across the street to Ada's.

I usually check in on her every evening. Not because she can't take care of herself, but because, I don't know, I like being around her, and she likes it, too. Tonight I am later than usual, and Ada's house looks dark. I fish my hand into her roadside mailbox and pull out a gardening catalog, a lottery announcement, and a copy of *Yankee* magazine, still addressed to "Mrs. Lawrence Bouchard," even though Ada's husband has been dead over thirty years.

I step onto the porch and pull open the screen door, which creaks under my grasp. Once Da' oiled it and it stopped creaking, but Ada and I both like it better when it's creaky because that's how you know someone's there.

"Ada?" I reach into the doorway to feel for the light switch. "Ada? *Yankee* is here."

"Don't worry, my dear. I won't tell." Her voice is closer than I expected, and it startles me.

"Tell? Tell what?"

"I won't tell your da' that you're in love."

I turn around and flip on the porch light. There is Ada, smiling broadly, sitting outside in the dark on her deep, slatted Shaker rocking chair, her porch-rocker she calls it, with a Pepsi-colored afghan tucked around her legs and a pillow embroidered with a tourist map of Nova Scotia on her lap. White horn-rim glasses sit over her deeply wrinkled face, holding comically thick lenses that magnify her mischievous blue eyes, giving her a permanent look of surprise. She shakes her head in a grandmotherly chuckle, forgiving and harmlessly supercilious all at once, as only an old woman can be.

"I don't know what you mean," I say. "In love? Who's in love?"

"My dear," Ada says. She points straight ahead from her chair to my driveway, a clear view of where Gabe just dropped me off. "With my glasses, I don't miss anything." She adjusts her lenses. "I know love when I see it." She smiles confidently, as if to say, *so there*. She is teasing me.

"Oh, Ada," I say, shaking my head. "I don't know about love. That was, I don't know. That was just a kiss."

"I don't believe that for a minute," she says. "If it wasn't love, you would have given up after the first try."

"What are you talking about?" I say, knowing exactly what she's talking about.

"But you gave it a second try." Ada blinks. "And a third. That was love. I know all about love. And I know that you are in love with that boy. He is in love with you. I can see it, plain as day."

"It's night, Ada," I say.

Ada looks down at her embroidery. "He is handsome," she says. "He needs a haircut, but most boys do. I remember him, Eva. He used to steal honey from my tree long ago. What is his name again?"

"Ada, stop," I groan. I can tell Ada's enjoying this.

"It doesn't matter," Ada says. "Love doesn't require names."

I look over at Ada, who is looking straight at me. "You are beautiful, Eva," she says, still smiling.

"I am not," I say, eager to change the subject. "What did you have for dinner, Ada?"

She stares at me for another moment, pausing as if to

say, *trust me.* "Leftovers. Sardines and rice and some carrot salad."

"Want to go inside?" I ask. "I can poke at your fire and put on some water for tea. The new issue of *Yankee* magazine is here."

After Ada falls asleep in her wingback chair next to the fire, I head home, say good night to Da', and go up to my room. I sit at the desk by my window and stare out into the starlit meadow beyond the barn. I don't think, or wonder, or fret. I just relive the kiss a million more times, and wonder if Ada is right.

Gabriel

AS WAS THE CUSTOM, THE BRIDE-TO-BE FILLED her father's table with a feast fit for a wedding's eve. A rich stew of *morue*, cod, in a savory broth made with pork knuckles and grape wine and summer herbs, with a great round loaf of crusty-soft oat bread to soak up the soup. Early-season pumpkins, cut into slabs and roasted on a rock in the vast fireplace, drizzled with honey and bonnyclabber and sprinkled with roasted wood-nuts. Cakes of toasted millet with freshly churned goat butter that Evangeline had mashed together with ruby-red brambleberries, the last and sweetest of the summer. Cider pressed from orchard apples, warmed instead of chilled for the first time that year. Thin slices of mutton cut from the glistening shank that spun on the trammel over the flame in the fireplace, watched over by Poc, who licked the hearth whenever a stray splatter landed there. Benedict, Basil, Gabriel, and Evangeline gathered around the table.

"The last time the ships came, do you remember, Benedict? Perhaps they did not kill us themselves, but because they were here, we lost lives. Important lives. My wife. My son. Our hearts suffered, my old friend." Basil sighed and swirled his cup of cider. "These, too, are enemy ships. All we don't know is precisely when, and where, they'll attack."

"Even if what you say is true, Basil, what would you do? Attack them first? We would lose. Flee into the woods? Extinguish our fires again and hide, and wait?" Benedict cleared his throat. "Shall we extinguish the flames, Monsieur Lajeunesse?"

"No," Basil said. "Not this time. We cannot."

"On that we can agree," Benedict said. "We have a wedding to attend to."

Evangeline walked over to the fire and reached in with her oven-hook to tend the mutton shank. Gabriel watched her go, half drunk as he was with cider and desire and the aroma of spit-roasting meat.

There was a loud knock at the door. "Monsieur Bellefontaine?"

Basil leaped to his feet. "Who goes?" he demanded.

Benedict chuckled. "At ease, Basil. It is the notary Leblanc," Benedict said to the room. "Here to sign the papers."

"Of course," Basil said, sitting back down sheepishly. "The papers."

"I also suspect he'll want to eat," Benedict said to Evangeline. "He always does."

Evangeline smiled at her father and opened the front door. "Monsieur," she said with a broad smile. "Welcome."

Leblanc gave a shallow bow. "My child," he said. "You grow more beautiful every day."

Evangeline gestured graciously into the room. "Please, come in."

Behind the lanky, wizened notary, the oldest and sagest man in Pré-du-sel, was his youngest son, Jean-Baptiste Leblanc, his fitted silken waistcoat stiff on his shoulders, his hair pulled into a wincing queue.

Gabriel rose to his feet slowly. He eyed Jean-Baptiste warily. What purpose could he have had in coming here?

"Welcome, René," said Benedict from his chair. "Please forgive this old man for not rising. The bones are simply too brittle tonight. You are both welcome. Please, take a seat near the fire to warm yourselves." He pointed to a pair of footstools hanging from pegs behind the doorway. "Are you hungry? There is mutton yet, and cider, and we have much to celebrate."

The notary and Jean-Baptiste each took a footstool and settled near the hearth. Gabriel sat across the room, on the windowsill by the kitchen, pretending not to watch every one of Jean-Baptiste's movements. Evangeline smiled at Gabriel, as if to say, "You, Gabriel, you are all I see." She poured cider into wooden bowls for the guests.

"How is business?" Leblanc said to Basil.

"Forget business," Basil said. "You have heard about the ships, have you not? I have seen them myself." At this, he glared at Jean-Baptiste.

"Ah, the ships," Leblanc said. He sighed. "Yes, Basil Lajeunesse. I have seen them," he said clearly. "We have."

"And," Basil said, turning away from Jean-Baptiste and back to the bespectacled face of the notary, "what do you think we should do?"

The notary didn't answer. He took a long sip from his mug and closed his eyes, as if his response were to be found behind his eyelids.

"Fight," said Basil impatiently. "We should fight."

"I do not agree," Benedict said. "What say you, Monsieur Leblanc?"

"I do not wish to fight," Leblanc said. "Bloodshed and

sorrow will surely follow if we choose that course. Still, we must be prepared for anything."

Basil slammed his hand down on the table. "We do not choose to fight," he said in his powerful deep voice. "But if God calls us to fight, we must!"

All eyes turned to the venerated Leblanc. A silent moment later, he said softly, "However fate directs us, I choose to believe that justice will prevail. Law will rule."

"Aye," Benedict said, raising his glass. "Let us drink to that."

"What law?" countered Basil. "We have no law that they recognize. They obey no law."

The notary raised his bowl of cider to the room. He took a slow, deliberate swallow, and began to speak.

> "Once in an ancient city, whose name I no longer
>   remember,
> Raised aloft on a column, a brazen statue of Justice
> Stood in the public square, upholding the scales in its
>   left hand,
> And in its right a sword, as an emblem that justice
>   presided
> Over the laws of the land, and the hearts and homes
>   of the people.

Even the birds had built their nests in the scales of the
balance,
Having no fear of the sword that flashed in the
sunshine above them.
But in the course of time the laws of the land were
corrupted;
Might took the place of right, and the weak were
oppressed, and the mighty
Ruled with an iron rod."

Leblanc's hands threw giant, flickering shadow-dancers across the wall as he spoke, slowly, in measured rhythms and soothing tones. Gabriel held his breath as Evangeline settled down next to him at the windowsill. He smiled at her, and she raised a seductive eyebrow. Gabriel, flushed, looked down and grasped his knees with his hands, willing them not to reach out and embrace her, as he so desperately desired.

"Then it chanced in a nobleman's palace
That a necklace of pearls was lost, and erelong a
suspicion
Fell on an orphan girl who lived as a maid in the
household."

Evangeline moved closer to Gabriel. He watched, unmoving and surreptitiously, as her right hand ascended from her apron and reached out to his own. Gabriel kept his eyes on the fire.

> "She, after form of trial condemned to die on the
>   scaffold,
> Patiently met her doom at the foot of the statue of
>   Justice.
> As to her Father in heaven her innocent spirit
>   ascended . . ."

Leblanc paused, for a sip of cider, or perhaps to focus his audience, or perhaps for some reason that only another storyteller could fathom. Evangeline's hand slipped under Gabriel's. She stroked the palm of his hand lightly. Gabriel flushed, but—desperate to show no weakness—did not move. He steeled his body and forced his gaze on the notary.

> "Lo! o'er the city a tempest rose; and the bolts of the
>   thunder
> Smote the statue of bronze, and hurled in wrath from
>   its left hand

*Down on the pavement below the clattering scales of
the balance,
And in the hollow thereof was found the nest of a
magpie,
Into whose clay-built walls . . ."*

Evangeline locked her fingers into Gabriel's. The notary glanced over at the betrothed, his eye pausing at their intertwined hands, and he smiled. Every eye in the room followed the notary's, and all smiled. Except for Jean-Baptiste.

74

". . . the necklace of pearls . . ."

Leblanc grinned widely now.

". . . was inwoven."

Leblanc stood up from his stool, squared his shoulders, and strode over to the windowsill where Gabriel and Evangeline sat.

"The moral, my friends," said Leblanc, because the notary never ended a story without a lesson. "The moral is this: Justice will always, finally, be done, no matter how imperfect its instillation. It is the way of the universe." He reached down and grasped the intertwined hands, engulfing them with his own two long-fingered hands, hands that had blessed such occasions before.

After all the mutton was eaten and the bone bestowed upon Poc, the notary oversaw the signing of the wedding papers. Gabriel's heart swelled with pride and affection at the sight of the notary's seal, willing Evangeline to Gabriel, and Gabriel to Evangeline, tomorrow.

Tomorrow.

Gabriel prayed that the tide would speed it here.

eva

I haven't heard from Gabe since we kissed.

I am worried at first, but I tell myself I'm being stupid and I just need to play it cool. Guys need space. Even if he got the note I left on his windshield, three days is not that many.

Maybe I shouldn't have left that note on his windshield. Maybe that freaked him out.

Whatever. It's not like I don't have enough to do to fill a day without hearing from Gabe. Like talk to my father, which I do when I get home from school today.

It's more like I listen while he talks. It's a thing we do. I pick up around the house and make meatballs for supper while he talks. Beef and bacon is Da's favorite kind of meatball, simmered in tomato sauce with chopped-up olives. While I'm cooking, I put a few sardines out on a plate for him.

We eat a lot of sardines at my house. It's almost like a political statement in Franktown to eat sardines. For a long time most of the jobs around here were at the sardine fisheries and packing plants. But I guess people stopped eating sardines out in the real world, and the plants started closing down. Now only one sardine company is still in business, Papillon Fish Co., so everyone in Washington County buys Papillon sardines like crazy, as if they'll keep the company afloat by eating more sardines. I doubt it will work, but who knows. Mrs. Sanders at Sanders' Grocery still gives you the eye if you don't pick up at least one can.

Louise hates them. She says they're *dégoûtant*. I guess most people my age probably agree. But Da' likes sardines and so do I, so I put some on a plate.

"Make certain that you see things, Eva," Da' says from the easy chair we moved into the kitchen last year so he can read the newspaper while I make supper. "The world, I mean. I've never been to New York City. I've never been to California. I've never been to Africa or China or London or Rome. I think that's where I'd want to go most, if I could go anywhere. Rome. Do you know why, Eva?"

I don't answer.

"Because it's old," he says. "Even older than I am."

"You're not that old, Da'," I remind him.

"Well, not as old as Rome anyway," he says, and the way he says it makes me wonder when he will die. The thought startles me.

I think about calling Louise, but I don't. I know she'd take pity on me and listen to me whine about Gabe all night if I needed to, but I also know that if Gabe called I'd ditch her in a second. So I decide that it's better not to get into a possible ditching-your-best-friend situation in the first place, and I don't call Louise.

Later I have a really hard time falling asleep. I try to figure out why Gabe hasn't called me yet. I start by listing all of the things I probably did wrong to make him not like me anymore. What really disturbs me is how many I am able to think of. Like, maybe he stopped liking me way back on the dock when he asked "down or up?" and I said up. Or maybe he thought he told me too much that day. Or maybe he didn't like the way I kissed.

Or maybe he never liked me in the first place.

I'm not sure when I fall asleep, or whether I really ever do, but I'm pretty sure I hear the first stone that hits my bedroom window early the next morning. Outside, the black sky is easing into grayish blue. Only the strongest morning stars are still visible; the big, lazy stars take their time fading in and out. Another stone grazes the window pane.

I shuffle over to the window. Another stone.

Gabe. I push up the six-paned window and stick my head out into the icy dawn. The dew is still airborne, wetter and colder than fog but easier to see through. I see a tiny glow from the sun, pink and speckled beyond the road to the east. A figure stands at the edge of the driveway. "Gabe?" I say.

"I need to see you," he says.

I can't see his face, but he is standing directly below my window in a black sweatshirt with the hood pulled up, not looking up at me, but looking down at the ground instead. His square, aluminum-framed backpack sits high on his shoulders. He swings his tent, bagged in nylon, in his right hand. His notebook hangs from the fingers on his other hand.

I need to see you.

"Are you all right?" I whisper, or shout, I'm not sure which. "Gabe?"

"I am going."

"What are you talking about?"

"Away, Evangeline," Gabe says. "I am going. Away."

"What?" I say. "Where? Away? Why?" Gabe doesn't respond, so I look for the answer myself. "Is this about Paul? Gabe?"

Nothing.

"Do you want to come inside?" I say. Da' sleeps heavily in the morning hours, and I know I can easily sneak Gabe in without Da' knowing.

Gabe doesn't respond. He just stands there, staring at the ground, his tent swinging back and forth. I expect him to turn around and leave, and the thought makes me panic, but he doesn't turn around. He just stands there, silently, shadowy, alone, as if he could vanish before my eyes.

We stay, deadlocked, me in the window and he below, for several minutes. How many minutes I don't know, but I do know I would stay just like that forever if it would keep him from walking away.

When the first direct ray of sun pierces the misty horizon at the end of the road, I gamble. "Wait there," I say. "I will come with you." I quickly pull on a pair of jeans and a sweatshirt and tiptoe downstairs, hoping to make it outside before he disappears into the mist.

Gabriel

"GOOD NIGHT, MONSIEUR," BENEDICT SAID TO the notary from his chair. "Good night, Jean-Baptiste. Gabriel, my son, will you bring the horses around?"

Gabriel glanced at Evangeline, who nodded and winked. "Just one of the family now," she whispered.

After Notary Leblanc and his son Jean-Baptiste rode off, Gabriel was able to breathe again. Evangeline pulled her cornflower cloak off the peg behind the door and locked her hand around Gabriel's wrist. She led him out the front door and into the small garden in front of the house.

"Evangeline," Gabriel said, falling into step behind her. "Where are we going? Our fathers . . ."

"Hush, Gabriel," Evangeline said. "Come." She wrapped

her voluminous cloak around her shoulders, hoisting its hood up over her head.

Evangeline led Gabriel to the gate, and around along the wall to the orchard. The fog had lifted and the air was now clear. A low, golden harvest moon poured muted light over the meadow, giving the landscape a magical, restless glow. The earth was warm underfoot.

Fourteen apple trees stood in three neat rows that each should have held five trees. As in most Cadian orchards, the ground beneath the trees was groomed and well kept, a close cropping of soft grass and moss inside a protective barrier of scarlet blueberry bushes. Evangeline stepped confidently in the dark—her feet knew where the ground was soft—and Gabriel followed her.

Poc appeared before them, leaping up to lick Evangeline's hand. Gabriel held out his own hand to Poc, but Poc met it with a growl. "Poc!" Evangeline said. "Quiet."

At the head of the orchard was a stone bench, a flat-topped boulder rising out of the ground, its surface polished smooth. Evangeline often sat there, to brush Poc, or to read to Benedict, or simply to sun herself. Gabriel knew, because he'd seen her do all of those things. He'd even spent the night on that bench, keeping silent watch over his beloved, knowing that she'd napped there earlier in the day.

Tomorrow, this rock would be transformed into an altar where they would kneel together before the priest and all the gathered citizens of Pré-du-sel and be married, their adoration for each other finally consecrated.

Tomorrow.

Evangeline leaped up onto the bench and held out her hand for Gabriel. A gust caught her cloak, sending it skyward like a sail. She lost her balance and stumbled a step, nearly falling off the rock. Gabriel scrambled onto the bench behind her, catching her shoulders. He steadied her from the back.

"My beloved." He encircled her with his arms, drew her head back into the cove of his shoulder, and locked his brown hands together across her chest. The wind was persistent and chilly, but they were warm together, and Gabriel was glad that, from this vantage, they could not see the ships that he knew were in the harbor. They stood in silence for several minutes, hearts beating apace.

"Gabriel," Evangeline said, her voice breaking in the wind. "Oh, Gabriel. What about the ships?" Evangeline spun around, her braid blowing wistfully in the evening breeze. "What will we do? Where will we go?"

"I do not know, Evangeline. I do not know." He grasped her more tightly, pulling her into his chest. "But we are stronger together. Do not be afraid."

But Gabriel was himself afraid.

Together they stood on the bench, solid and steady, facing the seaborne wind. Their hearts were uncertain together, impatient together, afraid and aware together, together, as they watched infinity over the edge of the bec, the boundless comingling of black sky and black sea and never-ending time, so unforgivably short.

eva

"Why are you limping?" I ask Gabe. I wince every time he comes down on his left foot, watching his shoulders tense with every labored, uneven step. "Are you in pain?"

Gabe, who hasn't said a word since this morning, since "I'm going away," doesn't answer. He just keeps walking. Limping.

Where we are, exactly, I'm not sure, because there were a few turns I lost track of. But we walk all day. For the first part of the journey we stick to the shoulder of the road, but after a couple hours, Gabe turns abruptly into the forest, disappearing behind a No Trespassing sign.

Da' has always told me that trespassing on someone else's land is one of the worst things you can do. "Land is as close to sacred as I know," he says. I remember him telling me that if you trespass onto private property, the owners could kill you and pay no price for it. You don't even have to be doing anything wrong. He says that one landowner in Aroostook County even tied up a trespasser and left him for the bears just for taking a pee on the side of the road near a No Trespassing sign.

But today, for the first time in my life, I ignore a No Trespassing sign. I disobey. I duck into the woods behind Gabe.

I will follow him anywhere.

86

We walk for several more hours, him limping ahead of me and me trying not to think about it, following a succession of trails through a dense forest of maple and tamarack, its soft floor padded with unknowable years of fallen needles and leaves. I know we are near the ocean because I can hear the surf off to the left, sometimes close, sometimes farther away. Through the shadows of the forest, I glimpse the ocean once or twice, brilliant blue and choppy white under the sun.

Twice we stop to rest. Gabe cuts chunks of salami with his pocketknife and hands them to me. He gives me his canteen and I drink.

Twilight falls earlier than I expect, but maybe I've lost track of time. It's kind of been like twilight all day, ever since

eva

Gabe appeared outside my window—not really daytime, not really nighttime. The light transformed with the hours, from golden to red to gray.

When Gabe stops, I'm not exactly sure why. Maybe he is just tired.

This spot looks like any other in this seaside forest. There are a few rocks and boulders tumbled around a tiny clearing in the pines. The trees are tall, some standing upright and some growing at an angle over the seabed, rooted in the outcrop that falls away just below the clearing. Looking at the watermarks, I guess that at high tide the water licks the rocks surrounding this clearing, but the tide is so far out right now that all I can see beyond the trees is mud and seaweed. A gull pecks at a crab in the muck. A few hundred feet across this shallow bay, I see more forest, perhaps an island or another peninsula, it's impossible to tell. Da' says there are thousands of miles of coastline around here, thousands of islands, thousands of ways to get lost. He says you could explore them forever and never really know your way around them.

Gabe drops his tent and pack and looks around the site. I watch him concentrate, and see the soft pulse of blood against his temples. He finds a patch of moss twenty feet in from the watermark. He touches it, wipes his finger against his jeans, and nods to himself. I follow his eyes, which follow a faint stripe of moss and sticks that winds up a steep embankment. Gabe follows the moss-trail up the hill, maybe twenty feet, then stops. "Here," he says out loud. I am surprised and relieved to hear his voice after his daylong silence. "A spring."

I climb up to him. Gabe fills his cupped hands with the bubbling springwater. I sip from them, holding his wrists to steady them. I sit, melting into the moss, and Gabe trots back down the hill.

In fifteen minutes, Gabe has transformed the clearing—pitching a tent, building a fire pit, starting a woodpile. He makes it look like someone lives here.

"There's a radio in my backpack," he says. "I wonder if we get reception."

I fish around in Gabe's backpack, feeling with my fingers for the radio. I feel his notebook in there. My hand closes around it. I wish I could read with my fingers.

I find the radio and hand it to Gabe.

"No, you try," he says.

I fiddle with the dials, but the only station I can get is a French-language pop music station from New Brunswick, Canada.

"Sorry," I say.

"Why?" he says. "This is perfect." He turns it up and we

listen to staticky songs we can't understand. I wonder what the staticky singers are singing about. I wonder if they're singing about love.

Gabe is quiet. Silent, actually, but I don't doubt he wants me here. He lights a fire with dried driftwood, and we sit by it, near each other but not touching, and we eat more salami, and an apple, which Gabe cuts up with his pocketknife and hands to me in pieces. When there's only one piece left, Gabe gives it to me. And then he moves next to me, brushes his bangs out of his face, reaches out and puts one hand around the base of my skull, my hair combed between his fingers. He pulls my face up and over to his and kisses me, solidly, insistently, unambiguously, completely—on the first try. I disappear into his kiss, close my eyes, and relax, letting him pull me in.

89

The kiss doesn't end for a long time. And then there is another kiss. And another.

"Are you in pain?" I ask. "Your leg, I mean."

"Nah," Gabe says. "Just twisted it I guess."

Later, Gabe climbs into the tent, which he's pitched on a level patch of ground near the high-tide line. I climb into the tent with him. Gabe smoothes out his down-filled sleeping bag and gestures me toward it. "Here, Evangeline. You sleep here."

I climb into the sleeping bag. He zips it up around me.

"But where will you sleep?" I ask.

"Outside," he says. "Under the stars."

"No," I say. "It's going to rain." I unzip the sleeping bag and hold it open.

Gabe looks at me, tilting his head, confused.

"Stay here," I say. "With me."

Gabe takes off his jeans and climbs into the sleeping bag. With me.

That night I sleep, I think, or maybe I don't sleep, to the dual rhythms of Gabe's slow, pulsing heart, so deliberate and clear, and the unmistakable creep of the tide, tossing tiny splashes closer and closer to the tent, slowly encroaching, eroding, rinsing away anything that came before. Feeding whatever is next.

Gabriel

"IT MATTERS NOT WHEN THE SHIPS ACT, OR whether they do," Gabriel said. He stood up straight, square, and confident on the rock-bench in the orchard under the stars overlooking the sea. He spoke in the old tongue, the one only the elders still used, and even then only at important ceremonies and sometimes in church.

"It matters not to us, my love. We are bound. Tonight, I know that I love thee, and that I wed thee, that as husband to wife I take thee, whatever chances or mischances befall us. With the infinite mine eternal witness, I swear to love and protect thee until death parts us."

Neither spoke for minutes, long minutes, until Evangeline whispered, almost inaudibly. "Not even death will part us,

Gabriel. We will be together forever," she said, touching her forefinger to Gabriel's lips. "Forever."

She descended the altar and settled at the far end of the orchard, protected from the wind. He followed her, and lay beside her in the moss. She curled next to him.

Evangeline's hands moved down Gabriel's shivering body. She caressed his chest, feeling his fevered, anxious heartbeat in her fingers. She grabbed at his midsection, his forearms, drawing his hands to her kirtle-laces. He felt her open his trousers, and with a single, eternal motion, she bent into and around him, encircling him with a slow, resolute strength, guiding him into her.

92

Gabriel lay, enraptured and unmoving on his back, staring longingly and needfully into Evangeline's dark eyes as she enveloped him. He lost his breath watching her movements and pulled her closer to him, deeper, moving together, until both he and she inhabited each other, until they both lay naked and silent under the stars and apple trees, kissing beads of sweat from each other's lips, folded together into Evangeline's cornflower cloak with Gabriel, softer now, still inside.

Together, they listened to the tide below, approaching, approaching.

eva

Gabe and I stay in the sleeping bag all night, sleeping and waking and sleeping again. Touching. Breathing. Feeling. Like the drive out to the lighthouse listening to Led Zeppelin, I never want it to end.

Morning is near. Gabe crawls out of the sleeping bag, pulls on his jeans, and steps outside the tent. I have been awake for a long time, listening to him breathe, and as soon as he's out of the tent I pull on my own jeans and follow him.

He turns toward me, buttoning his plaid flannel shirt. He runs his hands through his hair.

"Good morning," I say.

Gabe grabs my shoulders and presses me up against a birch tree. He kisses me, and I taste sleep on his tongue.

He is a part of my history now, after the way we held each other during the night, the way we moved together, the way he pressed into me, eyes and arms and hips. I'd wondered about that moment all my life, wondering when it would happen. I always worried that I'd be embarrassed, that I'd do something wrong, that it would hurt, that I would regret it.

But I wasn't worried last night. I was just *there*. And Gabe was there with me. And now, we are together, leaning against the birch tree on the morning after, and I have no regrets.

"See you," he says, and steps away.

"Where are you going?"

"I'll be back, angel," he says, and I believe him. He won't disappear. He can't. Not anymore. He turns and walks into the woods, limping like yesterday.

I stand against the birch tree and watch him go, listening to each fading footstep, each crack of a distant branch, straining my ears until every last sound of him has faded, until he is gone. The first rays of morning begin to stream into the clearing, but I don't move.

Later, I turn on Gabe's radio and set about straightening up the campsite, humming along to pop songs I can't understand. I air out the tent and rinse the dishes in the spring, then start to gather firewood to add to Gabe's pile. I don't know how long we'll be here, but you always need wood. Da' taught me that. I stay close to the campsite in case Gabe comes back.

I am a million miles from Franktown, a distance that blocks out the guilt I feel about running away in the first place. I know Da' must be frantic. I see him, still in his chair in the kitchen, watching the phone, as if staring at it would make it ring, afraid to call anyone to ask if they've seen me because he's afraid that the line will be busy when I call him. I see the dried tears, caking the corners of his eyes, and I want to reach out and wipe them clean.

But I am with Gabe now. Nothing else matters. Ada knows this to be true. She'll explain it to Da'.

I spend all morning and afternoon gathering firewood from the fallen trees in this part of the forest. I stack them precisely, twigs on one side, logs on the other. When I am finished and scoop water from the spring to drink, the pile of tinder is taller than I am.

At dusk I light a fire so Gabe can find his way back in the dark. I lay beside it to watch the flames and wait.

95

Gabriel

GABRIEL AND BASIL RODE WITH A MAJESTIC AIR, straight-backed in saddles and dressed in embroidered wedding coats crafted by Mademoiselle Gallan, the seamstress. Basil, father of the groom, wore a green coat with buttons carved from halibut bone. Gabriel wore black. Deep, pitch-black. The choice reflected the importance of the ceremony—true black was the most expensive color to produce, reserved only for high occasions. The coat was a gift from Basil, who'd been saving for it for years.

Gabriel averted his gaze from the harbor as they rode, lest he catch sight of the ships whose existence he so vigorously wished to deny. He felt for his birchbark in his foresleeve, lashed tightly against his veins. Its presence soothed him.

At the entrance to the Bellefontaine orchard, bathed in the cloudless, late-morning light, the assembled population of Pré-du-sel and the surrounding hills, every Cadian that Gabriel and Evangeline knew and many they did not, awaited the arrival of the groom and his father. Women wore wood lilies in their hair, brushing lint from their husbands' felt tunics. Children in knickers and sundresses wriggled through the crowd, hiding-and-seeking among the skirts and pantaloons of their elders. The older women tended the feast, baskets of bread and apples and pears and cheese laid out carefully on sheets of linen, and buckets of cider for after the vows were exchanged. Noisy groups of neighbors and relatives chattered and gossiped and laughed. None spoke outwardly of the ships, though all knew of them. All knew that this could be the last wedding in Pré-du-sel, but none said so.

Michael the fiddler, with a long shock of white hair and elastic legs and arms, struck a merry tune on his strings, a lively, vibrant melody that complemented the birdcalls from the woods and the squeals of laughter from the children. Garlands of autumn flowers were wrapped around the apple trees like ribbons on maypoles, and petals were scattered around the grass. At the sound of Michael's song, the guests scurried to the orchard, dancing in circles.

Père Felician looked up from the crowd to see Gabriel and

Basil approaching. He beseeched the crowd to part, to open a path in the middle of the apple orchard, a path to the stone altar where awaited Gabriel's intended. Abruptly, Michael stopped his jovial tune. The crowd answered with a rustle as they moved aside. Gabriel drew a sharp, strengthening breath and steadied himself on his horse.

The crowd parted to reveal the stone altar. There was Père Felician, who would preside over the exchange, his high-collared parson's cloak stiff and severe beneath his youthful face, his expression brimming with vitality and conviction, with delight in the moment and faith in the future. Benedict was there, too, balanced on his cane and draped in the embroidered stole worn by him, and his own father, and his father's father, on their wedding days, and which he would pass to Gabriel today.

And there, between the priest and her father, stood Evangeline, enrobed in layers of airy white silk and lace that flowed weightlessly from her veil to the graceful fluid sleeves that swayed below her hands to the richly embroidered overlay atop the skirt caressing the grassy ground at her feet.

Even through her veil, Evangeline's eyes of midnight sapphire, reflecting every color the sun showered on them, commanded Gabriel's notice.

Spellbound, Gabriel could do no more than stare, in

passion and thankfulness, astonished at the indescribable hues of her eyes, the eyes into which she, today, would grant him indefinite allowance to stare, endlessly, forever. Could it truly be? Gabriel willed this image of Evangeline into his memory, determined never to forget this moment.

Michael struck a new tone on his strings, a sober melody passed down from the ancients, the traditional wedding music that signified the arrival of the groom to collect his bride from her father. All eyes turned toward Gabriel and his father. They dismounted, handing their steeds over to a boy who walked them to the barn. Basil, beaming in the attention, smoothed flat his coat and led his son down the orchard-aisle, tipping his head at all he knew, which was nearly everyone.

Gabriel followed several paces behind, stalwart and steady and serious, eyes focused forward, only forward, grateful and humbled by Evangeline's adoring gaze.

eva

I am with Gabe again, only this time we are somewhere different, somewhere higher. There is no tide, no fog. We are in the mountains, high mountains I've never seen before, mountains above the trees. The peaks stretch ahead forever, and I know because I can see forever in every direction, and what I see is beauty, quiet and unchanging, no tides to wash away the past or the future, and Gabe's arms are wrapped around me, his notebook pressed against my chest, and we've come here together, to stay together, forever. And then I realize that we are not on the mountaintop, but soaring above it, flying, together, silently and effortlessly, the weightlessness of infinity surrounding us on all sides, lifting us higher and higher. As I rise, I look for Gabe, but he is gone and the sky is cold around me.

"AND DO YOU SO PROMISE, FOREVER?" ASKED
Père Felician. He stood behind the flower-strewn altar.

"I so do," answered Gabriel, kneeling before Evangeline.
"Forever."

Gabriel stood up and gingerly lifted Evangeline's veil.
Every corner of her face smiled at him. He kissed her, and
the crowd cheered. Michael's bow hit his strings, giving rise
to a cheerful tune.

And Gabriel, proud and complete, his beloved aside him
forever now, finally knew what it was to be alive.

eva

It is not until I wake up that I really begin to worry about Gabe. It is still night, and he is not back, and it is raining, hard. Not like raindrops, but like big, juicy chunks of water, splattering on the roof of the tent like water balloons. "It's raining cats, dogs, and fried fish," Da' would say. I am glad I moved into the tent.

I am not worried about Gabe's safety. Gabe knows the forest. If anyone can find his way through a storm, Gabe can. I am worried that he will never come back. Maybe he decided that he doesn't want me around. He wishes he hadn't brought me here. He didn't want us to be together last night, he hated the way I looked, the way I moved, the way I sounded. I try to remind myself how I felt this morning, leaning against the birch tree, unworried and certain.

I unzip the tent and shine the flashlight out into the woods. I gasp when its light catches a pair of sneakers, standing four feet from the tent.

Gabe's sneakers.

"Gabe? How long have you been standing there? Why didn't you come in?" I shine the light up at Gabe's face. "You're wet."

"I'm going, Evangeline," Gabe says, emotionless and stern and certain. "Away. Forever."

I slide on my shoes and step out of the tent and into the rain. "Gabe, what are you talking about?"

"I only came here to say good-bye."

"You said that yesterday," I say. "What's the deal?" My hair, suddenly soaked with rain, begins to mat to my face. "Gabe?"

Silence.

"I'll come with you," I say. I think. I'm not sure. I want to say it, and I want him to say yes.

"Not this time," he says. "No."

I point the flashlight at his sneakers again, then turn it off. "What did I do?" I say. "What did I say?"

"Not you," he says. "Not you."

"Is this about Paul?"

Gabe turns around and takes a few steps toward the woods before stopping. He shakes his head. "I failed him, Eva," Gabe says.

And I know, as well as I've ever known anything, that this time Gabe really is going away. He wants to disappear.

He walks not slow, not fast. I notice that he is limping more than before. His notebook peeks out from under his sleeve, wrapped around his forearm. And I just stand still and watch.

As his footsteps fade and his shadow is swallowed by the wet pre-dawn forest, my heart sinks and slows. I feel for my pulse in my wrist and I find none, and I wonder if this is what it feels like to die.

Gabriel

S UN GAVE WAY TO MIST, WHICH GAVE WAY TO A shower, reversing the usual order of things, but the wedding celebration progressed through the hazy seaborne spray. Gabriel held Evangeline's hand tightly while they danced, spinning her faster, ever faster, under the canopy of apple trees, her swirling skirts and his soaring soul caught up in the lively tune from Michael's fiddle and the clapping hands of the Cadians. All joined in the dancing, jackets tossed aside, the children skipping between the frolicking legs of the revelers.

Gabriel saw none of them. His eyes and mind were filled with Evangeline, spinning with him through the orchard, and there was no room for anything more.

The only man who didn't dance was Jean-Baptiste Leblanc, who stood beyond the orchard wall at the farthest crest of the bec, sullen, watching. Just watching.

Suddenly, as if from a giant's bugle, a shrill, ear-searing sound rang through the air, a blaring, disconsolate note so piercing and broad that Michael the fiddler dropped his bow and the dancing Cadians froze instantly, their flying skirts settling with a silent sway at their ankles. The air fell hollow and dead.

Wordless faces twisted in surprise and fear as each citizen searched the others for an explanation. Gasps gave way to whispers.

Evangeline darted to Benedict, clasping him in her arms. Gabriel turned his eyes skyward, seeking the source of the sound, and followed her.

"It is the sounding of the horns of heaven," said the pastor's wife. "Judgment day is here." A murmur ran swiftly through the crowd, culminating in the shriek of the seamstress. "The rapture!" she cried, filling the silent air with her frenzied call. "Oh, heaven!"

"You are wrong," shouted Basil the blacksmith above the panicked voices. "That song is not the angels calling us home. It is a song of ill. It is the New Colonists! They are here!"

Gabriel turned and looked over at his father, who was pointing at the woods just beyond the orchard. There, blocking the exit from the orchard, was a wall of sixty soldiers, muskets drawn, bayonets glistening, faces soulless and blank. They wore matching uniforms of close-cropped woven jackets, buttoned at the neck, with buckskin breeches and broad leather belts.

The blistering note rang again, slicing into the ears of the Cadians, drawing gasps and shrieks. Gabriel covered Evangeline's ears until it ended, then whispered softly, "Do not be afraid, my love. My wife."

"Attend!" shouted Basil, and he raced to the head of the orchard. "Gabriel!"

Confusion spun through the crowd now milling in quick, tiny circles as mothers searched for toddlers and old men tossed their hands toward the sky. "What will become of us?" "What do they want with us?" "Where is my baby?" Evangeline steadied Benedict, who was breathing heavily.

"Gabriel!" Basil shouted again. "To arms, my son!"

Gabriel stretched his head above the crowd, straining to see Basil. "Father!"

"Gabriel." Evangeline's voice was just a whisper, but it resonated in Gabriel's ear.

Gabriel took her cheek in his palm and cupped it for one

eternal moment. And then he tore his hand from hers and pushed his way into the panicking crowd toward Basil.

"Gabriel!" Basil shouted again. "To arms!"

But Gabriel, and everyone, knew that there were no arms there.

The wall of soldiers began to move. They stepped forward, in perfect formation and at an astonishing speed, easily surrounding the orchard in just seconds, muskets across their chests, bayonets raised. The Cadians crouched toward one another, condensing themselves in the center of the orchard.

"Cadians!" came a steady, booming voice, from a source Gabriel could not see. "Cadians, all. Please pardon our interruption." The murmurs quieted slowly. The voice had a strange accent, not entirely foreign but not a native speaker of the Cadian dialect. It was formal, polite, like he'd learned the Cadian tongue from books, not people. "Please, forgive us for interrupting what appears to be a lively set of festivities. We understand this is a day of celebration here."

Gabriel looked around the circumference of soldiers for the speaker. His eyes came to rest on the one intruder dressed, like Gabriel, in expensive black. His coat was stiff and square, with shoulders that sloped upward, giving the illusion of wings. Rows of silver buttons lined his chest in crosshatch patterns. His woolen breeches fastened at the knee with a silver closure. Two soldiers crossed their muskets in front of his chest as he read from a tablet. Gabriel guessed he must be the commander.

"We have been sent from the New Colonies by His Excellency Lord Governor Lawrence to welcome you and your land into his generous governorship, and he asks that all able male inhabitants of thirteen summers or more convene in the Great House for a formal meeting. Presently."

No Cadian moved.

"This way, please," the commander said, gently and politely and formally to the Cadians nearest him. "Thank you very much. Please."

"It's a trap," said Basil. "Beware."

Just then, a ruckus arose at the crest of the bec. Three soldiers had surrounded Jean-Baptiste Leblanc. Two soldiers lifted him by his armpits and a third began prodding him forward with the butt of his musket. Jean-Baptiste strained and thrashed against them, but the three soldiers dragged him down the bec and to the orchard with the others, tossing him onto the ground in front of the crowd. He quickly stood up and smoothed his jacket.

"Assemble the male inhabitants!" barked the commander, spitting as he said it.

109

"Yes, Commander Handfield," answered the soldier next to him. "Attention!" The soldier directed the soldiers flanking the head of the orchard to part. From the back of the crowd, soldiers began to bear down, nudging the men into a group and pushing the women and children aside to the stone wall.

Evangeline covered her father with her cloak, hoping to disguise him, to mask him from the soldiers, for he would surely die in their care, so frail was his body. A soldier tore at the cloak, revealing Benedict's face. "He is not able!" Evangeline cried. She pointed at his cane. "He is not able!"

The soldier pushed Benedict to the ground and walked on.

"Evangeline!" Gabriel shouted. A tall soldier grabbed Gabriel by one arm and jerked him away from her. "Angel!" He held out his other hand, but she could not grasp it before another soldier pushed her to the ground beside Benedict.

"Gabriel!"

The shower intensified over the bec, droplets running like tears down the cheeks of the gathered Cadians.

Evangeline squared her shoulders and steadied Benedict. "Take care, my husband," she said, though he could barely hear her. "Be not afraid, as I am not."

The rain, now a deluge, saturated the bec and all upon it, as the weaponless men were corralled into two lines and led away. Unprotected from the weather, they marched along the soaking, muddy trail down the back of the bec, sliding here and skidding there, trampling slowly toward the fate that awaited them at the Great House, musketed soldiers on both sides to keep any from flight.

Gabriel walked beside Basil and watched him simmer—surveying the guards, assessing their statures, recording their arms in his memory, silently moving his lips in running protest. Water ran down their noses, dripping into the trail ahead of them and soaking the tips of their moccasins. Gabriel fell twice, knocked down once by Père Felician, who slid into him from above, and once by a soldier who pushed him too quickly around a switchback and nearly swept him off the path.

III

It was two hours before the door of the Great House saw the arrival of Gabriel Lajeunesse and all the able men of Cadia.

eva

It takes me pretty much all day, but I finally find my way out of the woods, past the No Trespassing sign, up the road, and back to the house, where I find Da' in a wicked bad state. He hasn't slept in the two nights I've been gone. I feel even smaller than before.

"I am so sorry, Da'," I say, bending over the back of his chair and cradling his head after I feed him a warmed-up can of noodle soup for supper. "I am so sorry." He cries, just like he cried on my dead mother's birthday, and he calls me Evangeline, all the syllables, but this time it doesn't bother me as much as it did before, because I know how badly I screwed up, and I know I scared him, and if using that name gets him through being scared, then it's cool with me. I hold his head in my hands, watching the dusk fall outside the kitchen window.

Da' eventually falls asleep in his chair, and I call Louise.

"Where have you been?" she says, practically yelling. "Where are you? Did you hear?"

"I'm at home. Did I hear what?"

"Where have you been?" Louise repeated. "Were you with Gabe?"

"Yes," I say. "Did I hear what? What happened?"

"Where is he now?" Louise asks, urgency in her voice. "Eva?"

"I don't know," I say. I tell Louise about Gabe showing up at my house before dawn, about walking with him past the No Trespassing sign and into the woods, about the salami and the spring and the limp and the camp and the fire and the night in the sleeping bag and how he left this morning.

"So he didn't tell you?"

"Tell me what?"

"Eva." Louise's voice slows down. She says gravely, "It's Paul."

"What about Paul?" I say impatiently. "What now?"

"He's dead, Eva."

I freeze, the blood draining from my stomach to the floor below. My eyelids feel heavy. "He's what?" Dead? How could that be? Surely they found a donor for Paul. They did those operations all the time. Paul couldn't be dead. "How do you know?" I ask, and then I realize it's a stupid question.

"Eva, it happened two days ago."

I think back on the past two days, Gabe's strange appearance at my house in the morning, his silent walk, our night together, his disappearance, and then his second disappearance.

"Mr. Lejeune has been calling everyone in town constantly for the last two days looking for Gabe. No one can find him. Pretty much everyone is freaked out. Do you know where he is?"

I say I don't know, which is true.

Had Gabe known about Paul and not told me? Did he not know yet?

Or did he know everything? Is that why he left?

"Eva?" Louise is talking, but Gabe is all I can see, all I can hear. I know now why Gabe is gone, truly gone this time. I stare at my father, snoring in his chair, and feel the pain of this moment take over my body. It doesn't wash over me, it doesn't slice through me. It shreds me from the inside. This is a pain I've never felt before, a desperate, jittery pain that I don't recognize, that I can't trust. And it won't let me breathe.

But I don't want the pain to subside. Suddenly I'm nauseous with fear that it will go away, just like Gabe went away. And then I will have nothing.

I turn to look out the kitchen window. The first evening stars are rising.

"Eva?" Louise says.

"What?"

"Did you go all the way?" she says. "With Gabe?"

"What do you mean?"

"Just answer me, Eva."

I don't answer. I breathe a few times, and once my voice cracks when I open my mouth, but I don't form a word. Silence.

"I see," says Louise. *"D'accord."* And then she doesn't say anything for a long time.

I don't either. I hear a few drops of rain hit the windowpane, running lazily down the glass, distorting the early-evening view.

Louise talks first. "What kind of person disappears when his brother dies? Eva?"

"I can help him," I say. "I can find him. I have to find him."

"Eva, do you know where he is?"

"Oh, God." The words rise involuntarily from my stomach. *Oh, God.*

"You can't help him, Eva." Louise's voice is flat and serious. "You will only lose yourself trying, and no one will be able to find you."

Gabriel

WHEN ALL THE ABLE CADIAN MEN HAD FILED into the Great House and taken seats on the benches that lined the center of the common room, the front doors were bolted closed with a thud.

The commander stepped onto the small platform at the front of the room. Tall and slender and younger than half the soldiers in his employ, he had been protected from the rain by a canopy hoisted over his horse by six of his men on the trek down. Gabriel, bone-sodden, was insulted by the commander's dry uniform and clenched his jaw in humiliation and rage.

Gabriel counted eighteen troops surrounding the commander. He knew there were a hundred more outside.

The commander opened his tablet, cleared his throat, and read in a nasal, patrician voice:

"His Excellency Lord Governor Lawrence has resolved that the governing of this country shall be assumed by the New Colonies and the lands cleared of their current inhabitants, who shall be relocated thusly: To be transported to the Capital District, three hundred persons. To the Central Valleys, two hundred persons. To the Western Prairies shall be transported three hundred persons. And to Vieux Manan for holding until a final destination is determined, two hundred persons. We are ordered to use all the means proper and necessary for collecting inhabitants together for relocation. If we find that fair means will not do, we shall proceed by more vigorous measures. We are ordered to deprive any who escape all means of shelter or support by burning the houses and destroying everything that may afford them the means of subsistence. We are directed not to delay, and to use all possible dispatch to save expense to the public."

The commander rolled up the scroll. "Please remain here as we provision our ships and prepare for transport. You are now guests in this land."

Gabriel bit down on his lip, releasing a stream of bitter blood.

eva

After I hang up with Louise, I cross the rain-slicked street to see Ada. She is sitting on her porch-rocker under the front-door light, straining to stretch her embroidery canvas over its hoop.

"Hello, Eva," she says when I hit the first step.

"Hi," I say.

"Aren't you beautiful?" she says.

"Not really," I say. "New project?" Not that I'm really that interested. Gabe is missing. Paul is dead. I don't know what to think or where to turn. I guess this is why I came to see Ada. At least with her, I know what to do: turn up the television, fix a snack, help with the crossword, bring in the latest issue of *Yankee* magazine.

Ada ignores my question. "I never told your father where you were," she says, dropping the hoop into her lap. "I knew you'd come back."

"Thanks, Ada. But how could you have told him where I was? You don't know where I was," I say. I hold out my hand for the frame and the embroidery pattern. "I don't even know where I was." I stretch the pattern over the frame, smoothing and straightening it.

"Ah," she says. "But I know where your heart was. I know where it still is. And so do you."

"He's gone," I say. I lock the canvas into the hoop and hand it back to her. "Here."

"Then you must find him," she says. "You'll never stop loving him, you know. He'll never really be gone. My Gabriel is still here."

"Your Gabriel?"

"Yes, my Gabriel. My husband."

"You mean Lawrence," I say. Lawrence, her husband who disappeared in a storm over thirty years ago.

"I mean my Gabriel. Everyone has one." Ada takes my hand and puts it over her chest. "Eva, my heart is ancient. But it still beats for him. Only for him."

I look into Ada's glistening eyes. She is telling the truth.

"You must find him."

I know that she is right.

120

Gabriel

"Never!" shouted Basil, standing upon his bench. He tossed off his embroidered jacket and tore open the neck of his white linen shirt, flexing his powerful arms. "We will never leave our land! You will kill us first!" Basil thrust his fist over his head. "Rise! Cadians!"

Around the Great House, a few men's voices shouted in lackluster agreement. "No surrender!" But it was a meager battle cry. The able men of Cadia knew better. There were no arms there. There was no hope of resistance.

"Rise!" Basil bellowed again.

Three or four men stood up. Gabriel, crestfallen and hopeless and dizzy with panicked thoughts—of his village, of his future, of Evangeline—was not one of them. He did not rise. He simply sat and glared at the commander in the black suit.

"Rise, I say!" shouted Basil. "Death to these foreign soldiers, who seize our homes and our harvests! Gabriel!"

Gabriel moved to stand in obedience to his father, but before he could stand, the commander pointed at Basil. "Please escort the gentleman in the center to the isolation area." Three soldiers moved toward Basil, one pointing his bayonet, two approaching from the side.

"Death, I say!" Basil growled. He did not see the fourth soldier, bearing down on him from behind.

"No, Father!" shouted Gabriel. Basil turned for a moment to see his son stand, and in that second, the soldiers descended on Basil, tackling him to the floor. One pointed his bayonet at Basil's chest, the others held him. "Death to these foreign soldiers!" Basil cried, flailing against his captors, who pulled him to the front of the room, then through a doorway, which they closed behind them. "Never!" Basil's muffled voice cried out. "Never!"

122

The remaining soldiers cocked their muskets and aimed into the crowd.

"Oh, Father, forgive them," came a voice from behind Gabriel, pleading. "Forgive them." It was Père Felician, on his knees. "What is it that ye do?"

Gabriel let out a single, desperate sob. Then he, too, fell to his knees.

eva

It's nowhere near light yet, but I've been up for hours. Thinking. Preparing. Planning.

Ada's words keep bouncing around my head: *My heart is ancient. But it still beats for him. Only for him.*

I pack a flashlight, two apples, a canteen full of water, three tins of sardines, and a Coke in my backpack, along with Da's pocketknife and my rain poncho, only because Da' says you never know. I'm wearing Da's old fisherman's sweater as usual, and over it I pull on my brown corduroy jacket, the one lined with gray plaid flannel that Da' says isn't warm enough every time I put it on. I tie my hair into a ponytail and pull a baseball cap over that. I tell Da' I'm leaving early because I have to explain to the principal why I wasn't there on Friday. I hate lying to Da'.

"Do you want me to write the principal a note?" Da' asks.

I smile, and hug Da'. We both know that I've been writing my own notes since grade school. "I love you, Da'."

"And I love you, Eva."

Two hours later, I am standing at the No Trespassing sign at the edge of the woods. I look up the road, and back down, for any sign of a car or a bike or anything. Nothing. No one here to see.

I duck into the trees.

The change between the world under the open sky and the world under the trees is immediate and complete. On the road, I was squinting in the bright, white, mid-morning sunlight, but as soon as I breach the No Trespassing barrier, as soon as I'm three paces into the woods, the light is honeyed, golden, liquid. It dribbles like droplets from the gold and scarlet canopy of oak and maple and hemlock, diffused by the yellow-red leaves of ash. The light is dim here, but alive. Every wisp of breeze on a leaf overhead makes the light dance and ramble and speak.

I try to find the path back to the clearing where I left the tent, folded and packed carefully in its nylon bag and tucked into the woodpile to protect it from the rain, in case Gabe returned there and needed shelter.

But I can't find the path. I can't even guess at it. I walk

a half hour in one direction, then a half hour in another, probing the woods in every direction, certain I've seen this tree before, or that one, but it's as if these are different woods entirely, woods that I've never been in before.

But they can't be. These are the same woods Gabe brought me to.

I am wandering in circles, or I am heading straight on, east, west, I don't know. The ground rises and falls beneath my feet as I walk, through a thicket, around a marsh, over a log, across a stream, between boulders. I lean against a birch tree to rest and watch. Chipmunks scold me as I make my way through the trees. Birds scatter. Breezes swirl around me, alternating cold and hot and whispering words I don't understand, or perhaps I do understand—they are calling me to Gabe.

To Gabriel.

I answer back, or think that I do. "Gabriel." I say. I ask. I shout.

I cross a small clearing dotted with summer wildflowers— witchweed and wood lilies and Queen Anne's lace. Here and there the trees part overhead, revealing a patch of blue, brilliant against the flickering autumn leaves. A slow, squawking V of snow geese coasts across the sky. "Gabriel," they say, and then turn and fly the opposite way and I can't remember what season this is anymore.

I hear a branch snap to my left, and spin around. I see nothing. It happens again. I spin in the other direction and still see nothing. I stand and wonder, or maybe hope, that I am being followed. Another snap to my left. "Gabriel?" I say. I step backward. Another snap, this time behind me.

"Gabe?"

I nearly trip over the shivering, speckled fawn, curled in the nest of leaves and twigs assembled carefully by its mother. It blinks at me, with baby-doe eyes, struggling to pull itself to its feet, panicked in its tiny, frantic way.

Another snap. The mother. She must be nearby, snapping sticks to shoo me.

I step quickly in the other direction, knowing that a threatened doe can be dangerous.

A fawn? Wildflowers? But it is autumn.

I never see the doe, nor do I catch sight or scent of the sea, which should be all around me. I never find the clearing or the wood stack I so carefully built for Gabe, and when the light begins to sink from golden to amber to black, I realize I am going to spend another night in the woods.

I worry about Da', and hope that he found the sardines I left him on the kitchen counter.

Gabriel

For all the talk of a speedy embarkation, the men were kept locked in the Great House for many days. It didn't make sense to Gabriel. The invaders had every able Cadian man already. What could they be waiting for? What more could they want?

Perhaps they have been stymied by the Glosekap tide, Gabriel thought, and the thought gave him a moment of hope. It's always protected us before. Maybe it will foil their plan.

It was dark inside the Great House, day and night, and the rain, the pounding rain, had been unrelenting since the wedding. The room was thick with humidity and darkness.

The prisoners, for that is what they were now, had been fed once a day since their seizing, dense, dry, crumbly hunks of bread and a small cube of fat for each. A barrel of water was brought into the room twice each day, manned by a New Colonist soldier who filled the ladle and handed it to each Cadian in turn, who would drink straight from the ladle. The soldier allowed only one ladle to each Cadian.

"May I see my father?" Gabriel asked the water-bearing soldier when he reached the front of the line. "He is behind that door. May I take him a ladle of water?"

The soldier, who Gabriel could see was even younger than he, didn't answer.

128

Gabriel sat on the dirt floor in a corner of the room along an exterior wall, where a small space between the slats gave him a sliver-view of the fields outside. He guessed it was twilight, but it could have been dawn. There was just enough light seeping through the slats for Gabriel to trace with his finger in the dirt floor. He traced Evangeline's form, over and again, soft, strong lines that recalled her curves, her limbs. Gabriel imagined Evangeline as a deer and a panther and a porpoise and a girl, and his lines in the dirt recalled movements of each, and they nurtured a searing longing in his chest.

"Evangeline," he sighed through the slats as he drew. "Evangeline." He was not calling that she may hear, he was calling that somehow her soul might know that he longed for her.

Gabriel closed his eyes for a moment and remembered Evangeline, in her breeze-blown kirtle of blue and curly braid, feeding the chickens at her father's farm. He drew his finger through the dirt for a moment and closed his eyes again, now picturing Evangeline, staring with determination and love and anxiousness and desire into his eyes as she had the night they lay together under the orchard trees. Another blink, another vision of Evangeline, surrounded by the frothy gossamer of her wedding frock, her midnight eyes piercing like the jewels of an emperor, smiling at Gabriel, only at Gabriel, forever at Gabriel.

"Evangeline," he repeated through the slats. "Evangeline." He would repeat it for eternity, even if no answer ever came. "Evangeline."

"Gabriel?"

Gabriel stiffened. He wasn't sure he'd heard it at first. In fact, he knew he hadn't. He'd been hallucinating, that's all. Delirious. Hungry. Thirsty. "Evangeline," he whispered again.

"Gabriel!"

This time, the voice was unmistakable. It was she. His beloved.

Gabriel thrust his fingers through the slats into the rain. "Evangeline!"

He felt her fingers, wet and slick but warm and alive, grasp his through the slats. "My beloved," she said. "My beloved."

"You are wet," he said. "You must find shelter."

"I will not leave here, Gabriel," she said. "Now that I have found you. I have visited this place every night since our wedding, calling for you."

"What has become of Pré-du-sel?" Gabriel pleaded. "What has become of you, my beloved? Tell me!"

"They have kept us in our houses," Evangeline whispered. "We have not been allowed out. A new soldier has been sent to guard our exit each day. Father has not risen from his chair since the wedding. They say tomorrow they will gather us at the harbor and then transport us to the New Colonies."

130

"You must be strong, my love," Gabriel said, willing the fear from his voice, glad she could not see his despair. Suddenly, he was seized with a burst of energy. "You must escape!" he shouted.

"Not without you."

"Listen, Evangeline. You must take your father and escape."

"Impossible!" she said. "He cannot walk! And I will not leave without him and you both!"

Gabriel knew it was a waste of breath to convince her otherwise.

"Oh, Gabriel. Have you eaten? Have you slept?"

"I am well," said Gabriel, in as confident a voice as he could muster. "Do not worry, angel Evangeline. I am well, and Basil is strong. We will be together again soon. It matters not where they send us, or when; we will be together."

"You cannot deceive me, Gabriel. I detect in your voice that you are not well." She paused, and inhaled deeply. "But nothing, in truth, can harm us. We are one."

Gabriel pressed his cheek into the wooden slat, willing the feel of her cheek through the slat to his own. The warmth he imagined forced his eyes closed. "Here, Gabriel," Evangeline said. "I have brought you meat." She slipped two strips of leathered mutton through the slats.

"What about you, my love? Have you eaten?"

"I cannot," she said. "I cannot eat for worry."

"Then take this," Gabriel said, passing one strip back through the slat. "Let us eat them together, as husband and wife."

"My beloved," she said, and her words caught in her throat, and Gabriel could hear Evangeline, his sweet Evangeline, begin to weep, quietly, almost carefully, and though she couldn't see him, or perhaps because she couldn't see him, Gabriel wept with her.

eva

I am curled on a bed of leaves surrounded by trees, tucked under a sort of tarp I made last night from my rain poncho strung between two pines. The ground is hard, terribly uncomfortable, but at least it is dry. I have no pillow, and my hair is full of pine needles.

I got no sleep last night.

I get up and run my hands through my hair, working tangles loose with my fingers. I stretch. I fish around in my backpack for a toothbrush, but there isn't one. But there is an apple. It's my last one, but I bite into it anyway, the crispy flesh cool and sweet and clean on my teeth. Sun spackles sharply through the leaves overhead, and I realize it's already late in the morning.

eva

I remember how Gabe found the spring back at our clearing, and I look around for a patch of moss. Within minutes, I find a bubble of water spilling over a ledge, and splash my face with it and drink.

My poncho is wet with dew, but I roll it up anyway. I hoist my backpack over one shoulder and I start walking back the way I came. I think.

I walk for more than an hour before I reach the edge of the forest. But it's not the edge I was looking for. There is no road here, no sign that forbids trespassing. Here, the pines give way to a grove of white birch trees, and a few steps later the birch grove gives way to a sprawling meadow of green-gold sea grass and blueberry bushes. And beyond the grass, nothing. Only sky. The wind swirls around me, an ocean wind, not a meadow wind, and I can hear the restless, choppy surf in the distance. I realize I am on a bluff, high above the sea.

I walk through the grassy meadow, wind tossing my hair first into my face, then off to one side, then the other. It takes much longer to reach the edge of the bluff than I thought it would, thanks to rocks and pine logs hidden in the grass. When I reach the edge of the bluff, a monumental cliff falls abruptly below me; it is so high that I'm afraid to look over the edge.

When I do, gingerly, my stomach sinks to my feet and I feel woozy.

I lie down on my stomach and hang my head over the edge, safer that way. There are ledges on the cliff, and a few renegade pairs and trios of pine trees cling to its face. I toss a rock over the edge and listen, but its landing is drowned out by wind and distance and waves. I imagine daredevil kids climbing the face of this cliff, and dying for their foolishness in the frothy water hundreds of feet below, the salty waves slapping their bodies against the rocky outcroppings.

But I don't recognize this seascape, or any of the islands in this bay. I can't be that far away from home, can I?

I turn over and look at the sky. It is split in two—blue and clear and endless over the ocean, but dark to the west. Thunderclouds are gathering.

The wind picks up and I turn back toward the woods. I stumble on a rock. Only, it's not a rock. It's a stone wall. Crumbled, but still a wall of flat granite stones carefully stacked. I trace it around a large rectangle of land, a small plot. I walk its perimeter in just a few minutes.

At one end of the plot, surrounded by blueberry bushes and sea grass, I find a rock. A big rock, a boulder, with a level top so smooth it seems unnatural. Almost more like a bench, or an altar, something made by someone for something.

I sit on the edge of the stone and, feeling the warmth it's been absorbing from the sun, crawl onto it and lie down. A moment ago it felt like I was at the edge of the earth. Now I feel like I've been here before.

I don't even realize that I've fallen asleep until I wake up and see that the sun is low now, grazing the tops of the pine trees I emerged from this morning. I sit up quickly. Have I slept all day?

I stand up on the rock-platform to scope out the meadow for a place to set up a small camp. At the other end of the stone wall, I see two more large boulders. I could use those for shelter, I think. I gather my pack and walk over.

As I approach the boulders I see a small, crumbled building that reminds me of the old mill up near the lakes where Da' used to take me canoeing. He said the old mill was the oldest building in Washington County, which was saying a lot since Washington County had a lot of old buildings.

I walk over to the structure and run my hands along its stones and wonder what this building used to be. I wonder how old it is. I am amazed at the way the stones fit together, all irregular shapes but all perfectly fitted, like a jigsaw puzzle with moss growing from the seams.

I search in the wall for a place to wedge a stick to hang my poncho from and my fingers catch on something, something that doesn't feel as old as these walls, stuffed between the rocks. It is a notebook.

Gabriel's notebook.

Gabriel

AFTER FOUR DAYS OF HUNGER AND SLEEPLESSNESS and despair, the doors of the Great House burst open, and the once able Cadian men poured out onto the frosty meadow, tripping and stumbling and falling to the ground in the blinding sunlight. The days without sun had dilated their eyes, and Gabriel, with the others, squinted and covered his face to shield them.

Gasping not so much for oxygen as for this fleeting moment of freedom, false freedom, the men, weakened by darkness and hunger and captivity and fear, sprawled around the entrance of the Great House like seals tossed onto the rocks after a violent ocean storm.

Gabriel, lying beside a blueberry bush, looked through

his fingers, letting the light in slowly. The Great House, rising from the banks of the Manan River, stood beside him, looking over the harbor. Gabriel turned his head to see that the dock was surrounded by New Colony skiffs, sent from the ships anchored deeper out in the harbor.

They'd learned to navigate the tide.

"To your feet, Cadians," said a soldier. "You will now be escorted to your transports."

"Where is my wife?" Gabriel said to no one in particular. "Evangeline. My wife." He mumbled more than spoke, and struggled to stand.

"This way, please," said the soldier, prodding Gabriel to his feet with the butt of his musket. "This way." He pushed Gabriel toward a shuffling crowd of men.

Gabriel hobbled forward on weak, uncertain legs. "Father?" he said. "Where is my father?"

"My son," said a voice to his left. Basil.

"Father," Gabriel said. "You are here."

"Let me take your arm, my son," Basil said. "Let me follow you."

Gabriel mustered his last reserves of clarity and led his weakened father to the dock, following the others around him, eyes cast downward, spirits shamed and hopeless. It had taken only four days to break every able Cadian man, and here they were, broken, imprisoned, enslaved. Even Basil.

Gabriel carried his slumping father, struggling under Basil's weight but moving forward steadily with the crowd. So intent was he on not falling underfoot, on not dropping his father, that he barely noticed the women, children, and old men gathered silently at the dock. His eyes, reddened by darkness and desperation, nearly missed his beloved, disheveled and dirty but eternally lovely, bent under the weight of her own father, who leaned heavily on her sloping shoulders.

"Gabriel," she said boldly as he walked past.

Gabriel, ripped from his misery by her voice, spun to see the cornflower cloak of Evangeline. He reached out to her, almost unbelievingly. "My beloved!" he cried, breaking stride with the shuffling men and falling out of the line toward her. "My wife!"

"This way," insisted a soldier as he prodded Gabriel in the leg with the butt of his gun. "Return here, if you please." He took Basil from Gabriel's arm and pushed him roughly onto the dock.

Gabriel jumped over the soldier's gun and hissed. "She is my wife," he said gravely and determinedly. His eyes burned. "I will go to my wife."

The soldier whistled sharply, and suddenly four soldiers tackled Gabriel, pinning him to the ground. They flipped him onto his face and bound his hands behind his back with a spiky length of rope. "It is the troublemaker's son," one said. "Move him. We must hurry, or we will lose this infernal tide."

Two soldiers took Gabriel by the arms, lifted him roughly, pulled him across the dock, his unshod feet dragging behind him, and shoved him onto a skiff. The boat was flush with the dock, easing Gabriel's landing onto its floor, but not by much. An oarsman grabbed Gabriel and jerked him to his feet. Gabriel growled.

The oarsman quickly pushed off and began rowing for the ships.

"My son!" Basil shouted from the dock.

"Father," whispered Gabriel. "Evangeline."

The skiff rowed away slowly, carrying Gabriel, stroke by unhurried stroke, away from the dock, his father, his wife, his life.

A great cry came up from the collected Cadians still on shore, just as a fast fog licked across the land and drew an opaque curtain over the dock, the Manan River, and Gabriel's beloved Pré-du-sel.

This is the last I shall ever see of this place, he thought

as the cloud closed around him, and the sadness was so powerful and final that his knees buckled. As he fell, he saw flames striking through the fog, and realized that the fog was not fog, but smoke from a fire. They are burning the village, thought Gabriel in his delirium. It is over.

"Evangeline."

Gabriel slumped to one side, and toppled over the edge of the skiff and into the crystal-black ocean, as cold as an icy heart.

"Overboard!" yelled the oarsman. "Man over!"

"Worry not," answered the commander. "He is bound. He will not surface again. Row on. And proceed with the destruction of the dikes."

141

eva

I don't have time to decide whether to read Gabe's notebook. It just happens before I can think about it. I am transfixed by the first words in the notebook, sloppily lettered in Gabe's handwriting.

Evangeline set down her rake and untied her felt cloak of cornflower blue, draping it over the fence that enclosed the small garden in front of the small, square stone-and-log house. She pushed her linen sleeves up over her forearms, swiped her hair away from her face, and looked up at the low, wispy clouds above. Gabriel seized on the gesture, sweeping his charcoal across the sheet of birchbark.

I ignore the slowly building ocean breeze, the descending clouds, the fading afternoon light. I read intently, not caring about the time or the temperature, at turns enchanted and alarmed by the words in the notebook. I am swept away in the story, because it is Gabe's story.

I sit on the stone platform and read, straight through sunset and into the dense blue-dark of the Maine twilight. I read about Evangeline in her leggings of deerskin and kirtle of blue, and Gabriel clutching his sketch in pursuit of her beauty, and the rolling, golden land of Pré-du-sel, and of hotheaded Basil and fatherly Benedict and the threatening ships. I read about the wedding and the violence and the imprisonment and the separation at the docks. I read about Gabriel, who fell overboard but will not surface, because he is bound.

After the words *"Row on. And proceed with the destruction of the dikes,"* there are only blank pages. The rest of the notebook is empty.

Except for, tucked in the back, up against the spiral, a slip of paper that has been crumpled, then carefully folded, like a piece of rubbish retrieved from the trash can and reclaimed.

I unfold it. It is typed and ruled, like a third copy of a triplicate form, stamped: "Bangor Regional Hospital, Oncology."

Then it says: "Northern Maine's Best Cancer Care Facility."

Then it says: "Patient Name: Paul Lejeune, Franktown, Maine."

Then it says: "Indication: Lymphocytic leukemia."

Then it says: "Procedure: Bone marrow."

Then it says: "Donor: Gabriel Lejeune, brother."

I blink and read it again. Gabriel Lejeune, brother.

I stare at the paper for a long time, hypnotized, before a cold raindrop on my forearm startles me. I look up at the sky. I knew the clouds were getting thicker, but I am surprised at how gusty and dark it's gotten since I've been here. More raindrops. Are these really the first? My shirt is already soaked through. I'm still staring at the piece of paper, but I can't see it. I'm not sure how long I've been here.

So Gabriel knows about Paul. He was the donor. Was that why he limped? Was he recovering from the surgery? My heart hardens to think of the pain Gabriel must be carrying this day.

And then there is a voice behind me. "What are you doing here?" it says. The voice is deep, powerful, insistent. But not unfamiliar. I have never heard this tone before, but I know this voice.

I look up, but all I see is sudden darkness and flashes of light, distant lightning snaking through the thunderclouds, unrelenting flashes, one atop the other like a strobe light. Am I hearing things?

A massive crash of thunder overhead makes me jump. I turn, and suddenly the fuming sky above me roars, the storm now directly overhead, lightning illuminating the bluff, the sea, and the wild face in the wind staring at me.

"Gabe!"

Another strike of lightning, even closer now, illuminates the face again. It is him, only his face is different. Mangled, tight, angry like the sky, with streams of rainwater flowing from its planes.

"What are you doing?" he yells, and grabs the notebook out of my hands. "Did you read this?"

A gust of wind whips up behind him, catching his hair and blowing it into his face. Water swirls around him like an airborne whirlpool. I can't see his eyes, only his mouth, screaming, his neck red and bulging with tendons. "How did you find this place? Why are you here?" He seems so much bigger than I know him to be.

"Gabe! I—"

"How did you get here?" he wails, yelping, then begins mumbling, pacing. "No, no," he says. "No!" He looks back and forth, panicked. "No, no one is supposed to be here!"

"Gabe," I say, I whisper, hoping my voice will soothe him.

He stops for a moment and stares at me, body and voice shaking, and for a moment he is not an angry young man, just a child frightened by the storm. "It's not my fault," he says, voice shivering.

"Please," I say, holding out my hands, my hair plastered wet against my face. "Please." I want to shout but, like in a dream where your legs won't move just as you need to run, my voice fails me, and all I can do is whisper. "Please. Gabe."

"Do you hear me?" he shouts at me violently. "No one is to see this! No one is to know!" He suddenly turns and starts running, racing toward the edge of the cliff. He tears the pages from the notebook and tosses them into the air. They catch the violent wind, sweeping and spinning upward into the stormy night sky, shrinking as they're sucked, one after another, into the tempest.

"Gabe!" I whisper. "Gabe!" I race after him, not sure what he's going to do, only knowing that the cliff is there, just steps away, massive and unforgiving and slick, and after that there is nothing, only driving rain, black with rage.

"It's not my fault!" he yells.

I race, but I trip, and I crumple to the ground just as Gabe reaches the edge. "Gabe," I say. I get back up and stumble forward. "I love you."

eva

Gabriel Lejeune doesn't answer me, and I catch a rock with my toe, and fall again into the wet, cold grass, slowly, and before my head hits another rock and the blood starts to seep into my eyes, I see him disappear over the side of the cliff.

My last thought is to wonder if they will ever find us.

PART TWO

eva

I have accepted that Gabriel is gone. It's been a year and a half. I'm graduating today. Growing up. I'd better be used to it by now.

I know he's not dead. I would have heard about it if he'd washed up on a beach somewhere like the Felician girl. It would have been a big deal, like on the news and everything. "Local Boy Drowns in Tide, Residents Reminded to Wear Life Jackets." That kind of thing.

But I have no idea where he actually is. I spent months in those woods, looking for him, I guess. I knew how stupid it was, but I tried. I never found him, of course, and eventually I had to try to stop wondering where he was, to stop looking for clues, to quit listening to rumors. There's always another story: He's moved to Los Angeles, he's a drug addict in New York City, his father sent him to military school in South Carolina, he moved to Paris with a girl.

Wherever he is, he's not here.

When I do let myself picture him, or when I dream about him, which is harder to stop, he's always alone. He's never in the sun, always in the shadows, in the fog, in the forest. I can barely see him. But he's always carrying that notebook.

Gabe's father, Mr. Lejeune, is gone, too. Shortly after Paul died and Gabe disappeared, he moved to Boston. But then I heard he moved again, to Washington, D.C. Or somewhere. Who knows. Da' says that happens to families. Tragedy either brings them closer together or rips them apart. The Lejeunes were ripped apart. After Paul's funeral, they were like ghosts here. People spoke of Gabe and Mr. Lejeune, but no one ever saw them in Franktown again.

At the beginning of this school year, I even got rid of the quarter Gabe gave me, that day under the docks. His life's savings. Tossed it right off the edge of that same stupid cliff he disappeared over.

I can't believe we're graduating today. Louise has been all over me to wear striped tights and Converse sneakers under our graduation robes, which I protested against but finally gave in to because it was easier than explaining to Louise how refusing to wear stupid tights doesn't make me a party pooper. To be honest, I wanted to skip the whole graduation altogether, just blow it off, but when there are only thirty-three in your graduating class, people notice if you don't show up. I tried to use the excuse that Da' wasn't feeling well enough to come, which he wasn't, but Louise didn't let me get away with it. So here I am, walking across the stage to accept a rolled-up diploma from Principal Hawthorne, in a canary-yellow graduation robe over striped tights and Converse sneakers. Louise chose the tights—light blue and dark blue—I guess because we are both going to the University of Southern Maine down in Portland and those are their school colors.

I'm looking forward to college. I'm going to study pre-med. I don't know if I want to be a doctor or a researcher or what. I can't explain it, but I just want to learn how to fix things. Things like old age. Leukemia. Pain.

I wish Ada were here today. She'd be proud. But she hasn't been home since the New Year's Day blizzard, when she was picked up by the cops walking down Route 18A in a nightgown, bare feet frozen blue in the driving snow and ice. She spent a month in the hospital in Bangor, where they removed all except one of her frostbitten toes, and now she's living at Penobscot Pines in Brewster, where I guess she's going to die. I mean, it's not like you leave places like Penobscot Pines when you get better. People there don't get better. Ada knows it, and Da' and I know it, too. But we never talk about it, and everyone tries to pretend that it's no big deal. All Ada ever said about anything was once when I was telling her about how the crocuses were starting to come up back in Franktown, and she said, "I never got to say good-bye to my home." And then she smiled and shook her head, as casually as if she'd just missed a ringtoss at the Franktown Fair.

We go up to see her every two weeks or so. Sometimes she's embroidering or looking at *Yankee* magazine. Sometimes she's asleep. Sometimes she just sits there in bed, staring at the wall, with no expression at all. I'd be lying if I said it wasn't creepy when she's like that.

I think it made Da' pretty happy that I applied to do my pre-pre-med summer work-study at Penobscot Pines. I'll be answering phones, filling out forms, distributing activity schedules. Boring. But I'll get paid minimum wage, plus I'll get credits at USM. And I'll get to hang out with Ada, which I feel is something I'm supposed to do. I mean, we're practically related, and in a weird way she's one of my best friends. I haven't told her about my job yet. I want it to be a surprise. Da' said I can take his car for the summer, since he hates driving it anyway.

eva

It's going to be weird to be around all those old people all summer. Odds are someone will die while I'm there, which will freak me out. But I better get used to people dying if I want to study medicine. It's part of the deal. And I guess it's easier to be around old people who are dying than to be around kids who are dying. Like Paul.

Paul. He's the real reason Gabe left. If Paul had lived, if the transplant had worked, Gabriel would have gotten better. His father would have called him a hero. It would have been the best thing that could have happened to him. And to me, because he would still be here.

But that's not what happened. Paul died, because his body rejected Gabriel's gift. "Close but no cigar," as Da' would say.

Principal Hawthorne hands me my diploma and I shake his hand, then take my seat on the side of the stage. My canary-yellow polyester graduation gown catches a nail and tugs me backward. I tear at it, ripping the bottom seam of the gown. Principal Hawthorne glares at me. *You'll be charged for that,* he seems to say.

"Louise Letiche," Principal Hawthorne announces. "Valedictorian." Louise walks across the stage, shakes Principal Hawthorne's hand, accepts her roll, and smiles broadly. She yanks up her gown to reveal her tights, and the small audience applauds—except for Robert Manning, who barks "Go Wildcats!" which I guess means he's going to the University of New Hampshire.

It's no surprise that Louise is valedictorian. She is definitely the smartest girl in Franktown. Straight A's every semester. And I don't think she even studies that hard. She's just one of those people who knows the right answers all the time.

Ha. All the answers. I should have listened to her a long time ago. If I'd listened to Louise and not gone down to the docks that day with Gabe, if I'd never cried into his shoulder, if we'd never watched the stars come up over Passamaquoddy, if we'd never kissed, if we'd never spent the night together in that sleeping bag in the woods, maybe I wouldn't have ended up with a broken heart and twenty-six stitches in my head from tripping on a rock on top of that stupid bluff. I wouldn't have spent all those months after he left wandering the woods, even when the snow was past my ankles, looking for signs of him. I wouldn't have spent afternoons sitting up on the bluff, waiting for him to come back. I wouldn't have finally gathered up my courage and made the harrowing hike down the face of the cliff where Gabe had disappeared. I wouldn't have fallen the last twenty feet and broken my collarbone, and I wouldn't have had to wear a sling for the entire second half of my junior year.

156

I wouldn't have wasted so much time trying to find him. Or trying to forget him.

As I sit there, pretending to listen to Louise's speech, I'm surprised at the words that come to my head. *"Evangeline,"* *he sighed through the slats as he drew. "Evangeline." He was not* *calling that she may hear, he was calling that somehow her soul* *might know that he longed for her.* They are words from Gabe's notebook. I never memorized them. But they spring so easily to my mind. I wonder if Gabe ever finished the story.

Louise, whose summer plan is to wait tables in Bar Harbor (boyfriend shopping, she calls it), is up there talking about preserving the fond memories of high school and sticking together as we face the challenges of an uncertain future and having faith in our abilities and a whole bunch of other crap that I should probably be paying attention to, but then again I've already heard her practice the speech about forty-four times, and I personally don't really have that many fond memories of high school, and really I just want to get out of here. I'm glad high school is over. I'll be sad leaving Da', but really I just want to get going.

I look over to my right and see John Baptiste flashing a victory sign at me. He mouths some words, but I can't see them. Probably something dumb like "Come to my keg party later."

. . . .

Later, Louise and I do end up at John Baptiste's party, mostly because there's nothing else going on and Louise is determined to go out. Everyone's drinking some kind of punch, so I do, too. It tastes like Kool-Aid, sort of, only worse. I have a few cups and end up dancing to "Mony Mony" with John Baptiste. He grabs me around the waist and kisses me. "You don't even know how hot you are, do you?" he says. I kiss him back, but only a little peck, and only because I know Louise is watching, and only because I'm packing up Da's Dodge and leaving for Penobscot Pines tomorrow. I kiss him again.

158

I'm not proud of it, but I do it. Louise squeals and high-fives me. *"Très bien!"* she says.

I can't wait to get out of here.

Gabriel

SWEAT FLEW FROM GABRIEL'S BROW AS HE BOLTED awake, gasping for air.

The dream was the same dream he'd had every night for the last nineteen months, the short, awful dream in which he slips under the icy surface of Glosekap Bay, leaden, unable to move any of his limbs or even breathe. Paralyzed, he slips deeper into the night-black depths. He struggles to hold his breath, but eventually he loses the strength to resist and is compelled to inhale. Underwater, he opens his lungs to the cold, dark ocean and breathes in. The water flows into him, drowning him, chilling his body with frigid seawater, and he sinks faster, faster.

Just as he succumbs to the darkness he wakes up, rigid, sweating, and gulping air.

It was the same dream every night. Only this time, for the first time in nineteen months, Gabriel woke up not under the stars, but inside, under a roof.

Where was he? Gabriel struggled to remember.

His eyes scanned the room slowly. What little he could see in the near pitch-dark was bare, earthen walls and a dirt floor. He was the only thing in the room. He inspected every corner, first with his eyes, then with his hands, feeling for an exit. Faint, viscous light, dawnlike and sleepy, seeped in through a narrow, irregular slit carved out near the top of one of the mud walls. He found only one small entrance to his cave room, a planked wooden door about waist-high off the floor, set above a mud step. He pushed on it, leaning into the door with all his youthful strength, but it didn't budge.

Gabriel, who'd survived imprisonment in the Great House at Pré-du-sel, was captive once more.

He put together the pieces of the previous night when he was captured.

As the sun descended slowly into the gold-spun evening, Gabriel had come across a freshly killed rabbit in a game trap just up the bank from the river he'd been following the

160

last few days. The Lesser River, he'd heard it called, far to the north and west of his Glosekap home.

He'd entered the barren, boundless, tideless grasslands many weeks before, searching the skies for unfamiliar stars and following them, away from his Cadian homeland and toward, he hoped, his beloved Evangeline. With his birchbark and charcoal lashed to his forearms, he'd follow this rumor, or that one, listening to each hopeful story, each whisper, each assurance that the Cadians had survived, that they had settled together somewhere, just beyond here, or perhaps farther yet, across another horizon, ever closer.

In retrospect, he knew he shouldn't have taken the rabbit. The trap wasn't his. Even in the wilderness, that was a universal rule. But he also didn't think anyone would care about a rabbit. The trap was meant for beaver, he'd guessed. Or lynx. Not rabbit. Rabbits were plentiful, and valueless.

So he had taken it out of the trap.

He'd tried to reset the trap, that its owners might never know it had been tripped, but hunger clouded his brain and he couldn't decipher the mechanism. So he left the trap sprung, hoping its owners would assume by the tufts of rabbit fur that the quarry had escaped. Besides, the rabbit was already dead. It would only rot. So he gutted and cleaned it with his pocketknife, tossing the head and entrails into the bushes. Then he walked, carrying the rabbit by its hind feet to bleed it as he went.

Gabriel walked until the rabbit gave no more blood. There, in a small riverside hollow protected from the prairie wind, Gabriel built a campfire with driftwood and flint. He skewered the meager beast with a switch, and held it over the fire, watching the orange flames lick at the lean flesh, browning the meat and crisping the edges. After a few minutes of cooking, the sweet, gamey meat had a chewy, ropelike texture, tougher than fish or foul, the flesh legacy of a life spent running. Gabriel devoured it, scraping the bones clean with his teeth. Then Gabriel fell slowly, deeply asleep, curled beside the dying fire on the star-drenched bank of the Lesser River, fed full for the first time in days.

162

It was still dark when the four men came upon the sleeping Gabriel. They tied him before he could awaken and resist, binding his feet and hands with horsehair ropes, and gagging him with a wedge-stick. The men, strong-limbed and carrying the stench of range work, were speaking a language Gabriel thought he recognized, but could not understand. They dragged Gabriel up the riverbank to their horses. There, they tossed him into a small carriage half filled with firewood, with just enough room for Gabriel and a small, beady-eyed dog with splotchy gray and black fur.

The ride was long, and the potholes and ruts in the road tossed Gabriel like a dory caught in a stormy Glosekap tide, punishing and bruising his bound, weary body.

Gabriel thought bitterly that if he were caught in the Glosekap tide, at least he would have known what to do. He could read the tide. He could trust it. It would come in, then go out, then return. But Gabriel was far from the Glosekap and its tides. Nothing kept time here in this prairie land. Nothing here could be trusted.

The horsemen rode until the sun broke the morning horizon and raked across the midday sky. Without warning, one of the men shouted a command at the others, and the party came to an abrupt, jostling stop. Two of the men pulled Gabriel from the cart and tossed him onto the scrubby grass. One held his shoulders to the ground while the other untied his feet. They led him to a rise in the endless flatland, where the lead horseman pushed aside a brush-bush to reveal a small door built into the side of the low hill. He swung open the door and pushed Gabriel inside. Gabriel dropped heavily onto the dirt floor, landing just as the door closed behind him with a thick, heavy thud. Whether he'd been knocked unconscious by the fall, or just fallen asleep from the exhaustion of the ride, he didn't know.

Gabriel peered through the slit-window, out into the wide-open landscape beyond. He could see the morning light casting ghost-shadows among the rocks and shrubs. The grassland, so featureless in the expansive view, appeared dotted from Gabriel's confined vantage with orange and yellow flowers. Gabriel winced at the sight of them, so close were they in color to the wood lilies that grew in the gardens of Pré-du-sel and all around Glosekap Bay. They stabbed him with homesickness.

But Pré-du-sel itself was a ghost now, the structures burned to cinders and the dikes broken and the land rinsed by the same unfeeling, trustworthy tide that had also saved Gabriel's life.

Gabriel curled onto the floor and once again searched his memory, remembering that day, that last day of Pré-du-sel, the last time he'd seen Evangeline.

It was the coldest night he had ever known. Carried away into the sea after slipping off the dory in the harbor, Gabriel managed to shed his loose bindings and keep his head above water to breathe, just long enough to be washed ashore on the cove-side of Evangeline's bluff, out of sight of the ships. Shivering and soggy and sick, he then climbed up the rocks and into the woods, taking shelter in a bed of leaves just above the high-water mark, where he slept, perhaps for a day, perhaps longer, bone-cold all the while. When he awoke, he traced a spring for water, then walked back to the village, taking the hidden wooden path should any New Colonists still be patrolling the coast. It was a half-day's journey.

But Gabriel did not find his village. He found only a charred meadow, inundated by saltwater from the bay. The dikes were purposefully breached. The soldiers were gone. His village was gone. The Great House was gone. The dock was gone. Everyone was gone.

Evangeline was gone.

Gabriel climbed Evangeline's bluff to her house, expecting it to be burned as well. But, by miracle, design, or oversight, the Bellefontaine home was standing, humble and stalwart, and apparently unmolested.

A familiar bark in the distance betrayed Poc, loyal Poc, Evangeline's mutt. She would never have left him behind! "Evangeline!" he called, caught in a moment of youthful, doomed hopefulness. "Evangeline!"

Gabriel sprinted for the door, eager to burst inside, blindly expecting to see Benedict in his chair and Evangeline at her spinning wheel, but halfway across the bec, clarity befell him, and his gait slowed to a hopeless stumble. Gabriel knew better. There was no one behind the door. Evangeline was gone from there. Only Poc, suspicious, protective Poc, remained. He stood in the doorway, growling at Gabriel.

Gabriel stopped and looked a moment at Poc, until the growling subsided. He wondered how Poc came to be there alone, whether he evaded capture, whether the New Colonists refused him passage with his mistress.

Unoccupied, the Bellefontaine cabin still eerily pulsed with life. Neat stacks of firewood stood behind it. Ripe, unpicked apples shone in the pruned orchard. Chickens clucked in the henhouse. An empty bucket swung over the well.

166

Gabriel lowered the bucket into the well, filled it with sweet water, and placed the bucket on the ground beside the well. "Poc," he said. "Drink."

Moments later, Gabriel was inside the house, where the furniture stood in place. Benedict's and Evangeline's cloaks still hung from the hooks. Wooden bowls and steel knives sat on the kitchen bench. The bed was still rumpled from its last sleeper.

But the hearth was cold.

Gabriel wasn't sure if he'd decided to stay there, or if fate had decided for him. Winter was just a wind-whisper away, and there was no other shelter for some distance, many days' walk at least, if he even knew of a destination, which he did not. Days were shorter, and nights colder. Winter was no time to wander, and even Gabriel, desolate, abandoned, countryless Gabriel, knew how valuable this shelter would be.

He spent the next week gathering and stacking even more firewood under the lean-to behind the dwelling, enough for a winter. He scooped up the fallen apples from the orchard and pressed them for cider, setting it to ripen in the barrel by the hearth. He pulled up the onions and turnips from the garden and brought in the pumpkins, carefully storing them in the ground cellar. He insulated the chicken coop with dried grasses gathered from the bluff. And he faithfully fed and watered the ever-growling Poc.

167

"You don't have to like me, dog," Gabriel said. "But I'm not leaving just yet. You're stuck with me."

Gabriel fed Poc fish from the bay and crabs from the rocks and rabbits from the woods. One day, two weeks into the season of frost, he hit a deer with his bow and arrow. He cleaned it, butchered it, and froze the meat for him and Poc to gnaw on through the cold winter months. Together they slept in Evangeline's bed, where Gabriel would spend his nights imagining her beside him, enveloping him with her softness and warmth. He would resolve to find her, then resolve to endure his solitude, then reverse again. He would try to sketch Evangeline from memory, then chastise himself for failing to succeed. He would will himself not to cry. He would pray.

Gabriel remained in the cabin for five months. On the day the first crocus appeared, he gathered a satchel of belongings and walked down the bluff.

Poc did not follow, loyal to the cabin. This saddened Gabriel, who'd grown fond of his four-legged adversary, but he understood Poc's determination to protect the cabin, the only home he would ever know.

Gabriel walked thirty-six days before reaching the northern border of the New Colonies, where he crossed over undetected. Once within, he began to roam, friendless, homeless, helpless, and never certain of his route. He walked thirty-six more days, and thirty-six more, from ramshackle town to polluted city to pastured landscape, looking for signs of Evangeline. He disguised himself as a mute in one city, as a monk in another, as a simpleton in another, never speaking, only listening, listening for the sorrowful sounds of his native tongue, for news of the Cadian diaspora, of his father, Basil, of his beloved Evangeline. He chased rumors and wagon trains, ghosts and hope. He never gave up.

More than once, a campfire on a ridge in the distance

spurred him to walk all night, arriving at the site just as the coals choked forward their final, dusty offering of smoke.

Once, a rumor of a Cadian mission drew him south to the land of the crab diggers, where he found only the remains of a gale-tossed chapel, long abandoned by its shepherds. A glimpse of a colorful Cadian cloak, cornflower blue in a crowded city street, sent him racing through the throngs, only to find a Quaker maiden, not his beloved. A whisper of a Cadian huntress urged him into the deepest forest, but his quarry eluded him.

And now, the whisper of a Cadian community here along the Lesser River. Here, where Gabriel was now captive to men whose language he did not understand and intentions he could not know.

Gabriel sat back down on the floor of the dark, empty room and felt his pockets for a morsel. Perhaps from last night's rabbit. There was none. He would have to wait.

Wait and sleep. And dream.

eva

"Ada, it's me," I say. "It's Eva. I have your lunch." Ada is sitting on the small purple loveseat next to her bed, her head leaning back on a pillow embroidered with a picture of a seal. A month-old issue of *Yankee* magazine lies on her lap, opened to an article on Mount Katahdin.

"Eva, dear. Is it Sunday already?" Ada says.

In the months after she moved here, Da' and I used to visit on Sundays.

"No, Ada," I say. "It's Tuesday. I've come with lunch. You remember."

It would probably be easier just to say, "Yes, it's Sunday," but my supervisor, Mr. Lench, told me that you shouldn't do that. When the residents get confused or stop making sense, you're supposed to correct them.

"Lunch?" she says.

"Yes, Ada. I have lunch for you, just like I did yesterday. You remember. I've been working here at Penobscot Pines for a month," I say. "I'm living up at the Orrington Apartments across town. You remember. I was here this morning with your breakfast, and last night with supper, and yesterday at noontime with your lunch. You remember. You had chicken salad and cottage cheese and we watched *General Hospital* together."

"*General Hospital*?"

"It's on television, Ada. It's one of your favorite stories." I look at her yellowing hair. I decide to come back later and wash it with whitening shampoo after my shift. It turns her hair kind of blue, but that's better than yellow. "You remember, Ada."

"Eva," she says. "Beautiful Eva."

"Here," I say. I feed Ada a few bites of spoon bread that I slipped some maple syrup onto even though she's not supposed to have any extra sweets. She chews slowly, her lips curling around her teeth each time they come together. It's remarkable that Ada still has all of her teeth, but she does.

She brushed for her whole life with nothing but baking soda and water, and never even had a filling. If it weren't for the arthritis in her jaw and her screwed-up digestive system, she'd eat steak. But as it is, she gets spoon bread. And if I'm serving it to her, she gets a little maple syrup on it.

Sometimes Ada feeds herself, but not today. Today she just opens her mouth like a baby and waits. Each time Ada swallows, her eyes go blank for a second before focusing on the next bite.

After about half the spoon bread, her eyes glaze over. I know the look; it usually means she's going to check out for a while. That's what the nurses call it here. Checking out. When a patient stops interacting and just sits and stares at nothing. They don't seem to notice anything that goes on around them. They're not awake, but not asleep, either. It can last for just a few seconds, or for a day, and no matter what Mr. Lench says, you can't always get them to check back in. You can try all you want, but Ada comes back when she wants to come back, not before.

This time she's only gone for a minute or so, and when she checks back in, she checks in hard.

"Where has he gone?" she says, suddenly full of energy, her blazing blue eyes drilling into mine urgently. "Where is he?"

"Who?"

"Gabriel!" She's almost shouting, scolding me. "Where has he gone?"

I wonder if I could get away with pretending that I don't know what she's talking about. I'm trying to forget Gabe. But I answer her.

"I don't know, Ada. He is gone. He left a year and a half ago. You remember. I haven't seen him since. No one has. You know that."

Ada leans back in her chair. "Water," she says, and I bring it to her. I lie down on her bed.

Ada begins to tell me the story of her husband, her own Gabriel, her Lawrence, who served in World War II and Korea and returned home with honors, only to disappear in a nor'easter during a fishing voyage off the coast. They never found his body. Ada tells me about his funeral, and about how she never believed him to be dead, and how she never went a day without hoping he would come home and they would be together again. "Believing he'd come back is what has made my life worth living," she says. "He has not been here for over thirty years. But he's been here." She puts her hand on her chest and inhales slowly before whispering, "Forever."

When she finishes, I am not sure if I am asleep or awake for several minutes. I just lie on the bed and breathe.

173

"You must find him," Ada finally says.

"How?"

"I don't know, my dear. But where your heart has gone, so must your hand. It is the only way." She closes her eyes.

After a minute or so, I sit up at the edge of the bed. I say, "I tried, Ada. But he's gone."

Ada's chin falls to her chest with a sigh, and her breathing slows. It must be naptime.

"And I have a life to lead," I mumble to myself, propping up Ada's head with a pillow.

Gabriel

ONCE MORE, GABRIEL AWOKE WITH A START JUST before drowning in his dream.

But this time, all wasn't silent when he awoke.

An argument was in the air outside his prison. Gabriel could hear it through the window slit in the earthen wall. Three voices, maybe four, were talking over one another in a swell of heated speech, each voice louder and more urgent in succession. They spoke and shouted, one after the other and one over the other, in the language of his captors, familiar in cadence but unintelligible.

As the bickering continued, a new voice soared over the others, silencing all the rest. Gabriel sprung to his feet. It had been nineteen months, and he didn't recognize the words, but Gabriel knew the booming voice.

Basil.

Gabriel jumped up and looked through the window slit but couldn't see anyone, only prairie grass and clouds. The voices had been coming from around the corner. "Father!" he yelled.

The voices outside fell silent.

Gabriel pressed his face into the opening. "Father!"

"Gabriel!" shouted Basil. The voices rose again, all of them more frenzied now, but Basil bellowed louder than the others, interspersing his own language with theirs, layering word over word in ways that defied precision but, as Basil delivered them, were unmistakable and clear: *Open the door and release my son.*

"Gabriel! Attend, my son!" he roared. "Are you injured?"

"I am safe, Father," Gabriel yelled back. "I am unharmed."

Gabriel could picture Basil's veins popping on his neck, his eyes wide and tense, the corners of his mouth lathered. He spoke low now, careful and direct, with exceptional force. Gabriel understood none of the words, but they were powerful enough, and Basil's tone was powerful enough, to silence the others.

Soon, the door to Gabriel's earthen cell began to rattle, and then it swung open violently. Light poured in, and just

176

as on the last day of Pré-du-sel, Gabriel was blinded for a moment. He shrunk away from the door and crumpled against the wall, shielding his eyes from the onslaught of light.

"My son!" Basil said. "You are alive." He stepped down into the dark, earthen room. "Come. Where have you been? What took you so long to get here?"

"Father," Gabriel said. "I cannot see. The light."

Basil grasped Gabriel under his arms, drawing him up to his feet. "Come, Gabriel."

Gabriel rubbed his eyes as his vision crept back. He stepped through the doorway and out onto the grass, which stretched to every horizon. Blinking, squinting, he looked around for the other men, but there was no one else there. Only Basil.

He turned back to his father. "Where have they gone?"

Basil, whose hair had gone from black to gray but whose arms were perhaps even more powerful than before, stood before his son in dusty gaiters and a worn doublet of deerskin, and regarded him head to heel. "My son," he said, shaking his head at Gabriel's tattered breeches and road-worn shoes. He stepped forward and embraced Gabriel with a powerful, breath-stealing grip. "They have gone."

"Who are they?" said Gabriel.

"It doesn't matter. They have gone. We are alone now. They will require a fee, of course."

"A fee?"

"A fine, I should say."

"A fine? For the rabbit?"

"Nay. Not for the rabbit. For trespassing," he said. "They've requested four pelts and a barrel of cider. But I'll wait them out and barter them down to just a barrel of cider. They'll accept. They need me. I'm the only one in these provinces who knows how to shoe a horse." Basil tossed back his hair and laughed heartily. "You do remember how to press cider, yes?"

178

"Who are they?" Gabriel asked again, and more forcefully. "Tell me, Father. I have a right to know. Tell me now! Who are my captors?"

Basil regarded Gabriel sternly, then spoke slowly to his now-grown son, nineteen months and a lifetime wiser than before. "Only trappers," he said, "from the north. Their villages, too, were burned by the New Colonists. They have hardly any land, and you were on it."

"How do you know their language?"

"I don't," Basil said, dismissing the thought with a lordly shrug.

"But," Gabriel said, "they listened to you."

"They think I'm important, Gabriel, because I act important." Basil smiled. He boosted Gabriel onto his horse and, taking the reins, walked triumphantly upstream toward the river, leading the horse and quarry behind him. "Come. I will lead you home. It's just a short distance," Basil said. "Along the riverbank."

The white-blue sky was everywhere, unbroken by tree or hillside. Gabriel sat rigid in Basil's saddle and watched it through jostled eyes as the towering clouds glided silently by.

"Evangeline," Gabriel said.

"What?"

"She is there, too?"

Basil did not answer right away, but Gabriel also did not repeat himself. He knew that Basil had heard the question.

"You must forget her, Gabriel. Your future is here, with us. We are building anew. We will build, and we will multiply. Our defiance will be our language, our ways. They can move us, but we will persevere. We must. It is our only path. We must stay together."

"Evangeline." Gabriel's voice caught in his throat.

"My son," Basil said.

"I must find her."

179

"Gabriel. This land seems foreign to you, remote. But we are not so far away. Only five days from here, at the mouth of this river, the Lesser River, lies the port of Vieux Manan, where the New Colonists have assembled to fortify their garrisons. Once again, they seek to destroy us, to disperse us. We must prepare to defend ourselves against them, to protect our adopted land. We cannot allow ourselves to be evicted again. We have formed an alliance with the northern territories. Gabriel. We will fight."

Gabriel shook his head. "I must find her, Father."

Basil drew in a sharp breath as if to bellow, but he was silent. For several minutes, neither man said a word—not father, not son.

Finally, Basil broke the silence. "Evangeline is not important, Gabriel. Your place is here," Basil said. "You cannot go to find her. It is a reckless errand, dangerous and costly. And you are needed by your people. Honor is a higher calling than love, my Cadian son."

"She is my wife."

"No, Gabriel. She is not. You have been counted among the dead, along with Benedict Bellefontaine. You have been but a ghost to the Cadian people, a memory, a lost soul. And to Evangeline." Basil's tone was grave. "She has chosen another, and her wedding day is nigh, if not already passed."

"Impossible," Gabriel protested. "You lie."

"I do not lie, Gabriel. Evangeline is to marry Jean-Baptiste Leblanc in the city of Vieux Manan. Michael the fiddler brought the news when he arrived a fortnight ago."

Silence. Gabriel ground his teeth. Jean-Baptiste Leblanc. It could not be.

Gabriel closed his eyes. For a moment, he was back in his never-ending nightmare-dream, swirling into the cold black waters, drowning again in icy Glosekap Bay. Then, in a gasp, his breath returned and his eyes opened.

"I do not believe you, sir," Gabriel said. He reached around and took the reins from Basil and cantered ahead. "I cannot. I must go to her."

"But you don't know where you're going!" Basil shouted after him.

Gabriel only sped up. He had heard enough. Gabriel would follow the river to this city called Vieux Manan, and there he would reclaim his beloved. No one would stop him. Not even his father. He sped to a gallop.

"Gabriel!" Basil roared after him. "Attend! I will not lose you again! I will not lose you to this foolhardy quest!"

But Gabriel, itinerant, lovelorn Gabriel, did not stop for his father's call. He was closer now, closer to Evangeline than perhaps he'd ever been. He would not stop now, or ever, until she was again in his arms.

He sped along the path, the only path, toward a thicket of low trees in the distance.

eva

I am wicked late to Penobscot Pines this morning. I'm supposed to get there at eight o'clock and make sure that the files are ready for Dr. Wadsworth. She reads them over a cup of coffee every day at 8:15.

Dr. Wadsworth is very organized. She is also very skinny.

But I don't make it by eight. There are two reasons. The first reason is because I oversleep. The second reason is because on the way to Penobscot Pines, I get stuck at a railroad crossing while some endless freight train goes by, carrying massive stacks of Maine lumber to God knows where.

I sit there, listening to the too-peppy DJs on the morning radio talk show about the Boston Red Sox's winning streak, or losing streak, or something like that, and I zone out, watching the train flash by, car by car, *click-clack, click-clack.*

I stop watching the train and focus on the space between the cars, which flashes in and out of view in millisecond blasts as the train speeds by. I see, in those flashes, a beat-up pickup truck waiting on the other side of the train tracks, its half-rusted grill illuminated in quick pulses of light.

And I see him behind the wheel.

Gabe.

He's in the pickup truck, wearing sunglasses and a baseball cap. It is Gabe. *Clack. Clack.* He is unmistakable. *Clack.* With every flash, a scene emerges from between the cars. Gabe and I by the dock. *Clack.* Gabe and I at Quoddy. *Clack.* Gabe and I kissing in his headlights. *Clack.* Gabe in my sleeping bag. *Clack.* Gabe disappearing over the cliff.

I stare, motionless, through the racing rain.

But when the train ends and fades into silence, there is no truck on the other side of the tracks. There is no Gabe. He is gone.

I sit for a moment, not moving, until the car behind me honks. I look into the rearview mirror and wave. "Sorry," I say, knowing the woman in the car behind me can't hear.

When I arrive at 8:25, Dr. Wadsworth calls me into her office. I sit on one of the folding chairs in front of her

184

desk. She gets up from her chair, walks around the desk, and perches on its edge, standing before me, stern and serious. I know I'm in trouble.

"I'm sorry, Dr. Wadsworth," I say, looking at my knees. "I'm late." I close my eyes and wish this moment were over. "There was a train."

"Eva," she says. "Eva, listen to me. Ada died last night."

"What?" I look up, almost to her face but not quite, stopping at her pendant, a sterling globe on a chain that lies across her rippled sternum. "She was fine yesterday," I say matter-of-factly, like I know something.

Dr. Wadsworth doesn't repeat it, because she knows she doesn't need to. I heard her. *Ada died last night.* That's it. No embellishment, no *I have bad news,* no *I know how you must feel.* No candy or sugar at all.

Ada died last night.

Just like that.

"Ada died last night," I say.

Dr. Wadsworth just nods.

I shouldn't be surprised. Ada was old. She wasn't well. She'd been preparing to die for months. Ever since she got to Penobscot Pines.

But I didn't think it would happen last night. She seemed so lucid yesterday, so energetic. Most people around here die

185

after coughing for two weeks, or after breathing through a machine for a month while their families haggle over what to do with them, or something.

Not Ada. Ada just died.

I'm sad. I think. And scared. I have to tell Da', and he'll get all weepy, and we'll have to figure out what to do, a funeral and whatnot, and then I'll have to do it. Now I'm mad. Once again, I'm going to have to do everything. Is it my fault my father's so feeble? No. Not my fault.

Then again, maybe it is. Maybe I made him feeble. Maybe I just wore him out. But I'm the one who has to suck it up and do everything.

I wish I could ask Ada what to do. But Ada died last night.

"I think you should go home," says Dr. Wadsworth. She picks up her clipboard and pen. "Go home this afternoon. Spend a few days with your father. I'll see you back here on Monday."

"What about my shift?" I say hopefully. "I'm on the schedule, see?" I point to the dry-erase board on the wall. I'm clearly down for work today and tomorrow.

"Go home, Eva," she says. And then she gets up and leaves the office to make her morning rounds, which will be one stop shorter than yesterday. I wonder if Dr. Wadsworth still gets sad when a resident dies, or if it even affects her anymore. She's worked here over ten years.

eva

I wonder how long it will take them to fill Ada's bed.

The ride home is a slow procession of station wagons from Massachusetts and Quebec, filled with Maine-gawkers covered in mosquito bites and sunburns, screeching to a halt at every ice-cream stand and any sign that says CLAMS, and asking questions like, "Is this lobster salad authentic?" The drive should take two and a half hours; today it takes five.

Normally, this would be misery. But I'm in no rush today. I don't mind. It's not like I'm all that eager to get home.

I spend the time rehearsing what I'm going to say to Da'.

"Da'," I'll say. "Ada died last night."

A few miles after Machias, the traffic dissipates. Before long, I'm pretty much the only one on the road. I roll down the windows and cruise under the brilliant-blue summer sky. The pines overhead whiz by, dropping splotches of sunshine onto the road as I take the small rises and curves one after the other, slow here, then fast, then slow again. I take out my tired ponytail and let my hair whip across my face and eyes, and wonder if I'll stop when I get to Franktown or if I'll just keep driving forever.

When I get home and yell hello and walk in the door and see Da' sitting in his upholstered armchair by the window overlooking the street, smiling at me with serene, bloodshot eyes, I realize he already knows.

"Come here, Eva, my girl," he says.

"Da'," I say. I stand beside his chair and put my hand on the armrest. He has one of Ada's old quilts wrapped around his legs.

"Eva," he says. He reaches up and pulls me down onto his lap and pulls my head onto his shoulder. "You were her angel." He reaches up and strokes my hair with his fatherly fingers, brushing it off my cheek softly. "And now, she will be yours."

I don't cry. Instead, I fall asleep. Right there on Da's shoulder.

188

Gabriel

AT THE BASE OF THE THICKET WAS A SMALL, stony river-beach. Four birch canoes lay in a jagged row on the rocks. Gabriel quickly tied Basil's horse to a tree, dragged the sturdiest-looking canoe into the shallow water, and without pausing or looking back for his father, paddled, swiftly and powerfully, into the depths of the slow-moving Lesser River, trusting the current, slow and languorous here, rapid and swirling there, to guide him downstream to the seaport of Vieux Manan, to Evangeline.

He wove handily through the drooping boughs of the ancient willows and the tangles of incessant river weeds, steering around the shifting sandbanks and rocky islets, paddling with newfound strength and energy, beyond the edge of the vast western grasslands and into the teeming forests beyond, where the river's shadowy aisles grew darker and closer, and the moist, thick air flowed like syrup into his lungs.

Gabriel's rhythms as he rowed coaxed his thoughts toward Evangeline. He imagined them together in the one-room log-and-earth cabin he'd built on the pastured hillside above Pré-du-sel, framed with chestnut and stone, and roofed with thatch from the marshes. The wood of his oar recalled the oak he'd hewn into her cider press. He pictured the long bench, the ladder-back chairs, even Evangeline's footstool, all carved by Gabriel's own hand. Gabriel had honored his wife's wishes and built a kitchen window over the low sink basin, overlooking a sloping field of wildflowers, oxeyes and hawkweed and white clover. There was a sturdy shed with room for four goats and a dozen hens. Farther on, an orchard of saplings, and the living waters of Glosekap Bay.

190

The house was his greatest expression of love for her. But it was now just a pile of ashes and cinders. Evangeline had never seen it.

Softly the evening came. Gabriel drifted and wept alone in the twilight. His shoulders collapsed and sobs of exhaustion and desperation skimmed across the river. "Are you so near to me?" he cried to the riverbanks. "Have you dreamed of me?" His voice carried through the fireflies gleaming on the riverbank, and into the dark caverns of the night forest.

"I will build another house for you, my beloved. I will build another life for you. This is my vow." As he swore, he felt the first raindrop on his forearm.

The storm came in slowly, with the markings of a shower, not a torrent. The heavy drops fell into the dark river around him, and Gabriel, though he knew he should find cover, swelled with determination, not prudence. He paddled more deeply in the rushing water, keeping a steady rhythm as he rowed: "Evangeline, Evangeline."

The storm grew only stronger, drenching the oarsman and conjuring up a formidable, swirling headwind, but Gabriel didn't stop. His goal was forward, and though already drenched, he rowed on.

191

Each stroke of the oar now brought him nearer, ever nearer, to her.

eva

"It's too late. It's done."

Da' is still stirring the coffee that I set down in front of him at least ten minutes ago, as if the half-and-half isn't yet mixed in. I managed to convince him to get out of that easy chair and sit at the kitchen table while I fix us a couple of sardine sandwiches, open-faced with cheddar cheese melted over the top. I find some coleslaw in the refrigerator, too, which I sniff and set out. The pale green cabbage and faded orange carrots match the cracked floral vinyl tabletop. "I've already sold it," he says.

"But Da'," I say.

"Half of it is yours," he says, still stirring his coffee.

"Half of what?"

"The house. The land. The money."

"Da'," I say. "If you've sold the house, where are you going to go? Where are you going to live?"

"That's not all," he says. "Ada's property is ours now, too."

"What?"

"Yes."

Ada has maybe a couple dozen acres. I never really thought about what would happen to her property if she died. I guess I figured she had some nephew or cousin somewhere who would show up, probably bummed out that they had to deal with trying to sell it off.

"What do you mean, her property is ours?"

"Ada's lawyer called me after we took Ada to Penobscot Pines. He said she would be leaving pretty much everything to me, and you. He says that if we found the right buyer, the land could be worth a decent price."

"No kidding," I say.

"It will help pay for school," he says. "You won't have to borrow as much."

"But Da'. Where are you going to go?"

"I can't stay out here, Eva." He sounds so old when he says it. "Come here. Look." He points out the kitchen window to the lawn. The grass outside hasn't been cut since I left a month ago. The rosebushes are disheveled and brown. The fields beyond are choked with weeds. Only two chickens are left after a fox attack last week.

"It is too much," he says. "Even the barn is falling apart. The roof needs replacing. The loft is full of mice."

I know that he is right. He can't stay here. But I can't imagine him living anywhere else. And I can't imagine anyone else living here.

"Are you sure, Da'?"

He is silent for a minute or two, letting his watery eyes dart left and right before closing them behind heavy lids. "Our story here is nearly finished," he says. "And you are grown. It is time."

He stops stirring his coffee.

Later I call Louise and ask her if I can come to Bar Harbor for a couple of days before I go back to Penobscot Pines. She says yes, of course, and I drive down to meet her after her shift at Blueberry Fields Cantina. She steals a bottle of champagne from behind the bar and we drink it on the beach, where the midsummer moon is full and the sand glistens. Louise tells me about her latest beau, Gaston from Montreal. "He wears the tiniest bathing suit!" she says. *"C'est tragique."* We laugh, and then I tell Louise about Ada dying, and how the last thing she told me to do was find Gabe.

eva

I laugh out loud, but maybe I laugh too hard, because Louise doesn't laugh with me. She just shakes her head.

On our tipsy bike ride home, I fall off my bike and skin my knee, and the raw pain of it makes me feel so small and motherless and lonely. I am glad I am with Louise, but I really wish Gabe were here with me instead, because he was once small and motherless and lonely and he would understand.

But Gabe is gone. No matter what Ada says.

When I wake up with a headache I tell Louise that I've decided to stay in Bar Harbor for the rest of the summer. I call Da' to tell him I'm going to wait tables with Louise at Blueberry Fields until school starts. Even though it means sacrificing my credits from Penobscot Pines, I'll make a lot more money.

When I call Dr. Wadsworth to tell her my plans, I can tell she is annoyed. But then she says that if she were in my shoes she would probably do the same thing.

Gabriel

IN THE MIDST OF A GREAT STORM, IT IS IMPOS-
sible to quantify time or distance or damage. What occurs in
the dark swirl of weather is unseeable, its effects unknowable.
Decisions are made without forethought or pretext or
wisdom. Actions and decisions are only justified later.

And so it was that Gabriel, though equipped with the
knowledge and experience and will to shelter himself from
nearly any storm, indeed to thrive in it, ignored his better
judgment, giving in to his obsessive quest and pressing on
through the great storm now howling around him.

He paddled, facing the driving rain and racing wind.
Streams of water collected in his hair and flowed down his
face, and his eyes squinted to slits, but he forced his small

canoe through the oncoming wind and waves and darkness, digressing as much as progressing but undeterred and single-focused and determined to move ahead, whatever lay in his path. Obstacles did not matter. Nothing mattered, only rowing. For it was only rowing that would bring him to Vieux Manan. Only rowing would bring him to his reward, his beloved.

Her image appeared before him, hanging in the air just above the bow of his canoe, beckoning him ever forward. "Come, my love. Come." He saw her, curls cascading softly around her shoulders, midnight eyes shining with comfort and love. He imagined her alone, waiting for him, quiet and content, carefully tending to their house, to the goats and cider and garden, scanning the seascape of the bay for her beloved like a sea captain's widow in the years after battle. He would not disappoint her.

He imagined her with friends, among Cadians in a village as beautiful as Pré-du-sel, nay, in the very village of Pré-du-sel that belonged to them, that they belonged to. He imagined the stories she told of his devotion, his persistence, his never-ending quest to return, and to return to her the life he'd promised.

He imagined her mourning his reported death, a demise the others, perhaps even Père Felician, wisely but wrongly told her was certain. He imagined her in an embrace, a passionate embrace with Jean-Baptiste Leblanc, resigning herself to the apparent truth of her new future. He imagined Jean-Baptiste's hands on her. He imagined them lying together. He imagined them petitioning Père Felician to release her from her past entanglements and allow her to marry Jean-Baptiste.

The storm, stronger now, spun his boat in directions unknown. But Gabriel, fighting current and gale, rowed even more furiously.

eva

USM is a big enough school that they don't do dumb small-school things like not allow you to choose your own roommates, which meant all Louise and I had to do was ask the admissions office and they let us room together.

We spend our first couple of days getting the dorm room organized: cheap carpet from the thrift store, posters of black-and-white photographs (*"très chic"*), a tiny refrigerator. We signed up for classes—two requireds (American Studies and English—ugh) and four electives (I choose Organic Chemistry, Biological Ethics, Basics of Anatomy, and French). I picked French because Da' always wanted me to learn it since that's what his parents spoke. I know I'm going to hate it.

On the morning of our second breakfast, I see Gabe standing in front of us in the cafeteria line. His back is to us, but the rolled-up sleeves of his flannel shirt and his worn jeans are unmistakable. I stare for a minute, or maybe a hundred, until he turns around and I realize that it's not Gabe. It's hard to shake off, but Louise refills my coffee cup over and over until I do.

Part of the pre-med requirement is an on-site work-study program at a hospital or hospice or other health-care provider. I get my first choice for assignment—assisting a group of nurses at the Cumberland Medical Center, which is one of the best hospitals around. I'll be in the Palliative Care Unit.

Palliative care is where they send you if they can't cure you. Kind of like Penobscot Pines—you don't really get better and go back to regular life. They just try to keep you quiet and comfortable. They don't bother trying to fix you, because they can't. By the time you get to palliative care, they've pretty much tried everything they know.

My shift at the Cumby is twice a week, Thursdays and Fridays, from five P.M. to midnight. The job is mostly sitting at the nurse's station, waiting for something to happen. I answer phones when they ring and file paperwork when they ask me to. After my first few shifts, they started having me deliver mail and things to the long-term patients. By last night I was answering patient calls to see whether they really needed a nurse or whether they were just having trouble with the television remote control or needed a refill of water or whatever. If it didn't involve touching the patient or the medical equipment, I was allowed to take care of it.

The nurse's station where I sit is surrounded by a low wall, separating the "pit," as they call it, from the rest of the hospital. It's Friday, so the hospital is pretty active all afternoon, with visitors and patients and doctors and nurses and lab techs and fighting families crowding the hallway. Families fight a lot in hospitals.

At 7:45 I take my thirty-minute lunch break. It's really supper time, but they call it lunch here, so whatever. I go to the cafeteria in the basement. It's wicked depressing down there. I stand around looking at all the options along the self-serve tray-slide line, the Salisbury steak and the chicken fricassee and the seafood chowder and the Jell-O, and I must have seemed really indecisive and pathetic, because finally the guy behind the counter, who's wearing a name tag that says MAX, tells me to get the chili. I'm skeptical, but he says it's the only thing there he'll eat. I scoop myself a bowl, he hands me a chunk of corn bread, and I pay my $1.70 and sit in one of the industrial-orange booths to eat.

Max is right. The chili—black beans and red beans and

ground beef and tomato sauce—isn't that bad. And the corn bread is fine, too, especially with an extra slather of margarine. I eat alone.

Later, after my break, the hall lights go dim and the hospital slides into quieter hours. Visiting time ends at nine o'clock, and people start trickling out well before that, intent on keeping normal lives while their mothers, sisters, babies are waiting for their diseases to either fade or finish them off. I sit at my desk at the nurse's station and watch them go, without looking up.

By ten o'clock, there's almost no one in the hospital. My shift doesn't end for two hours, so I crack open my Organic Chemistry book. I'm already behind.

Gabriel

UNDER A STORM-FILLED SKY DARKER IN DAYTIME than he'd ever known it at midnight, Gabriel, disheveled of mind as well as body, drove his canoe forward into a furious downward stairway of storm-fed rapids.

Rain turned to hail and drove down from the sky, swirling in deadly whirlpools, first this way, then that way, sideways and upward together through the air, slapping the surface of the river like buckshot, boring into Gabriel's hardened flesh like stones. Blood flowed from his limbs and eyes, washed by the water as quickly as it was drawn to the surface.

Gabriel shouted in defiance, still paddling forward as his canoe bounced and tumbled its way over the rapids and rocks, tossing him aft and fore and nearly capsizing his craft.

His weary muscles were surging with determination and foolish faithfulness, and he struggled to stay on his knees, digging his oar deeper and more forcefully into the river with every stroke, until his boat drove hard against a boulder in the whirling stream, rupturing the shell and sending a thunderous crack through the whistling, groaning winds.

Gabriel, drawing on strength that came not from his body but from a force greater than the one he commanded, did not waver as water seeped into the doomed hull, but he paddled on, determination giving way to madness, shouting her name, "Evangeline! Evangeline!" even as the river swamped the canoe and began to pull it apart and below the swirling surface.

It wasn't until the canoe broke cleanly in half that Gabriel stopped paddling and released the boat, and his own body, to the raging current, swept away into the depths of the swirling, blackened, hail-pocked water.

Gabriel held fast to his oar to stay afloat. With a few frantic strokes he maneuvered through the wind-whipped rapids to a steep, slippery bank under a row of pines, bullets of hail pummeling his head. Tossing the oar aside, he pulled himself, slipping here, catching himself there, bloody-fingered and sweating in the rain, up the shining rocks and away from the river, climbing onto a ledge under a jagged overhang. In another instance he would have judged this ledge too precipitous, too dangerous to stop on, but Gabriel was saturated, with exhaustion and delirium and rain, and so there he stayed, wet and cold and shivering with fever. He would regain his strength and wait out the pounding deluge.

The rain cascaded from the sky like a waterfall, spinning in the day-night above and around him, stifling everything else on earth to an unheard whisper. The storm lasted through the night and into the next day, a day unmarked by sunlight.

Gabriel, sapped of strength but not of hope, laid his heavy, sodden head on a curled arm and slept deeply and still, as only the dead can do.

eva

I fall asleep at the nurse's station, textbook cradling my head like a pillow. I dream about the night on the bluff when Gabe went over the edge. Only, in my dream, I don't lose consciousness after I hit my head. In my dream, I float away from the bluff, and watch Gabe climb down the cliff in the rain, clinging to the narrow trail that exists there only for thrill-seekers and death-wishers, and I watch him climb into a dory and push out into the head-high, cone-shaped waves, chopping black and green and blue through the bay, tossing the dory from crest to crest. In my dream, there is no tide sweeping in and out through the harbor, only violent clockwise swirls in the storm-churned water, leaving paisley patterns of foam across the surface of the bay. Gabe rows between the waves, away from the cliff, away from the dock, as pages from his notebook flutter around him and into the sea, where they sink and disappear.

When I awaken, at first I'm not sure why. There isn't a voice coming over the loudspeaker or anything. The phone isn't ringing. I look around, but there's no one here. Only fluorescent lights and a bunch of files. I take a deep breath and look back at my textbook and struggle to remember what I was reading before I passed out on top of it.

"Are you OK?" It's Cammie, one of the night nurses on duty, walking by.

"Can you watch my station for a minute?" I say. "I have to go to the ladies' room." Which I don't, really. I just want to get up for a few minutes and take a walk.

Cammie takes my seat and I walk down the hall toward the bathrooms. I push my way through a pair of swinging hospital doors, finding myself at the head of a long hallway, nearly empty except for an IV tower and vacant wheelchair about thirty feet ahead. Patients' rooms line both sides of the hallway, plastic file-holders mounted just outside each door, a clipboard swinging from each one.

I carry on down the hallway. I've never been in this part of the hospital before. It's surprising to see all the patients' doors closed, rather than open. I peek into one. It's empty. I peek into another, and another. Empty. All the rooms in this hall are empty. This is strange, I think, because the other nurses have been complaining about the shortage of beds, about how the administration has been talking about doubling up and tripling up patients, even those who've requested and paid for single rooms.

But all of these rooms here are empty. It's eerie.

The hallway ends at another set of swinging doors. I push through them.

I find myself in the emergency waiting room. It's quiet here; the only sound comes from the television flickering above clusters of chairs spread across the tiled floors. There is a candy machine on the left wall, next to a hot chocolate machine and a table stacked with tattered magazines. Wide, sliding glass doors, activated by an electric welcome mat, open into the parking lot beyond. During the day, the doors whisk open and close rhythmically, as patients and others enter and exit, but tonight they stand silent, reflecting the fluorescent room back into itself. To my left, a pass-through window opens into the intake desk, where I see two attendings playing cards. They don't look up. I scan the walls for signs to a restroom, which I didn't really need in the first place, but now that I've come all this way, I figure I might as well pee.

Suddenly, sliding doors sweep open. A figure in a hooded

black sweatshirt comes busting into the room, arms wrapped tightly around himself, face obscured by his hood. He lunges toward the intake counter, moaning, but his sneakers trip up underneath him and he collapses to the floor with a thud.

"Help!" I yell.

The two attendings jump up from their cards. "Are you all right?" one yells as he leaps through the pass-through. I point at the man, now lying facedown on the floor, deadly still. "Call security!"

I race to the hooded man, reaching him before the doctors. His body is tense, rigid. I crouch down and strain to turn him over.

He is bleeding from the mouth. His eyes are wide, dilated, glazed. His arms are wrapped around his own torso with a desperate grip.

And against his chest is a notebook.

It is Gabe. His eyes begin to roll, and the world beyond me, beyond us, disappears.

Gabriel

GABRIEL COUGHED HIMSELF AWAKE AND OUT OF the drowning dream, the incessant dream that had plagued him since the destruction of Pré-du-sel.

It took a moment of squinting through the sunlit mist to remind himself where he was. And why.

Evangeline.

Gabriel was hot, as if with fever. And he was also cold, exposed here, in this foreign mist. Shivering and sweating together. But the rain and wind had ceased.

He coughed. His skin felt cold and clammy against his wet, tattered clothes. Gabriel looked around for his waistcoat, then remembered that he'd lost it in the river.

"Evangeline," he said to the mist. His voice wavered and cracked with fatigue and thirst. "Evangeline." He couldn't be certain if he said it aloud, or merely thought it.

The last thing he expected to hear was an answer, but an answer came. It was a voice, a girl's voice, humming or singing, he could not discern, so muffled by the mist.

"Evangeline," he called again, weakly. "Evangeline!" Heat raged through his temples and his head drooped from his limp neck. Gabriel wiped the cold accumulation of sweat from his forehead.

"Evangeline?"

The lilting, ethereal voice, beautiful and melodic, came from the brush just below his rock.

Gabriel, soggy and dirty from the splattering storm, sat up and, hitting his head on the overhang, looked dizzily down into the brush. There, surrounded by mist, was a girl, a tall girl he saw only from the back, with dark, wavy hair and powerful shoulders. Deerskin leggings covered her legs, and there were leather moccasins on her feet. Her body was turned away from him.

"Evangeline!" he said again. He leaped off the rock and landed heavily at her feet. He stood up and, wobbling, threw out his dirty arms to embrace her.

Only, when he closed his arms around her, she wasn't there. He was hugging only himself. And the music of her voice became the disconsolate silence of misery.

"Evangeline," he whispered as he collapsed into the brush, arms wrapped around himself, shivering with fever. He did not see the rainbow above him, half formed but vibrant with colors of violent yellow and red, for as soon as he rose up from the brush, the rain began again.

eva

E vangeline."

Gabe chokes up a column of blood with my name.

Then, with a shudder, Gabe's body goes limp. His eyes roll violently, blue turning to gray turning to black. His lips quiver. I take in a sharp breath, and hold it.

Activity swirls around me. One of the emergency room guys pushes me aside. I lose my balance and tumble backward, sitting down on the hard tile floor. "Backup! We need transport!" the other one yells toward the swinging doors. They crouch over Gabe, one pulling apart his eyelids and shining a flashlight into his eyes, the other bowing his head to lay his ear on Gabe's chest. "Stat!"

A gurney comes crashing through the door, pushed by

a middle-aged nurse with an intense, breathless stare. The three hoist the shivering Gabe onto the gurney. His notebook falls to the floor, unnoticed, as they race toward the swinging doors. And Gabe is gone again.

"Gabriel," I say, sitting alone on the silent tiled floor.

I pick up the notebook and, in the lonely flicker of the fluorescent lights of the waiting room, I begin to read.

Gabriel

THE GRAY AND GUSTY STREETS OF VIEUX MANAN were rich with the scent of ocean and wood fires and fish, aromas that Gabriel, even in the opacity of his fever and desperation, had detected well before he arrived.

It had been three days since the stormy night on the river, three days since he'd lost his boat, three days of dizzy, dirty trudging, following the bramble-filled banks of the Lesser River, gathering scant fistfuls of wineberries and leaves of wood herbs for sustenance and thirstily sipping the churned-up water from the river, a source that in long-ago days of lucidity and wisdom he would have dismissed in favor of an easily found spring, but that thirst and carelessness had driven him to. Three days of walking, of losing, then regaining his footing, of feverish faith and obstinate determination, of visions of a reunion with Evangeline, had brought him to this place, this muddy collection of docks and storage garrets laid on a cockeyed grid by the sea. Vieux Manan.

Gabriel wandered with uneven steps and uneven thoughts through the deserted lanes at the outskirts of the compact town, where weathered row houses leaned awkwardly against each other in crooked repetition. Tiny plots wedged between blocks held shelters for goats and horses and small vegetable gardens. But there were no goats. The plots were fallow.

Not a single person crossed his path as he entered Vieux Manan. The city felt empty, but Gabriel knew that it was anything but: Behind the shuttered windows and bolted doors were certainly warm, dry citizens, driven to their hearths by a week of lingering rain.

He was desperately hopeful that behind one of those doors was his beloved, his Evangeline, but his heart beat with trepidation that even if he found her, she would be wrapped in the arms of another, of Jean-Baptiste Leblanc. He spit at the ground in disgust.

It mattered not, he told himself. When he found her, after these months of wandering, of searching, of yearning, then

Jean-Baptiste Leblanc would simply disappear. Everyone would disappear. Only Evangeline and Gabriel would remain. It was this vision of a happiness, a complete, eternal, soul-encompassing happiness, contained between the two, that gave him energy even as his fever drained him. It was this vision that renewed his desire to breathe, to move, to search, to find.

Evangeline.

Gabriel, waterlogged and weary, his shoulders hunched in the storm, was grateful the wind had begun to abate. He guessed haphazardly at the direction to the sea, to the harbor, to the docks near which the center of the city would likely be. From there he would canvas the streets of this unfamiliar city, spiraling his way outward to its perimeter, and back in again, until he found Evangeline. He would search in the streets, peek in the windows, speak and shout her name with whatever strength he might find. He was nearer than ever now.

He would find her.

And they would, again, be together. And his wandering, their journey, would finally end. He would be home.

Gabriel walked through the city, drunk with his mission, exhausted and blistered but unwilling to stop. Unable to stop. He held himself up on the brick and wooden walls of the structures for balance, stopping every few steps to look behind and ahead of his position. He squinted into every uncovered window, but saw only gray, cold interiors bereft of people. The warmed hearths or busy drawing rooms or families gathered for song or mealtime or prayer lived only in his imagination.

If the city wasn't deserted, it was asleep.

Unsure of his feet, half clad in torn moccasins, Gabriel slipped frequently into one or another of the carriage ruts that dug through the saturated city streets, staining his already soiled garments with cold, wet dirt.

Gabriel walked for hours, covering a muddy block or a muddy mile, he knew not which. Thoughts came stubbornly, words not at all, only his beloved. Only Evangeline.

"Evangeline," he muttered through the slowing raindrops. "Evangeline." But the streets were silent.

After a time, a long time, Gabriel crossed paths with a pair of journeymen, weighed down with rusted scythes and darkened visages. They did not greet him. Later, an old woman, with holes in her skirt and dirt on her cheeks, pulled at his jacket and hissed, "Pestilence. All will die!" Gabriel heard but did not comprehend the woman.

Gabriel had the harbor of Vieux Manan in his sights when from behind him came the rumble of horse hooves, approaching rapidly. "Attend!" exclaimed the driver with a booming voice as Gabriel jumped aside. He turned to see a young man driving a pair of horses, black hair flying behind him in wet tendrils, straining to hold the reins of the galloping steeds. "Attend!"

The horses, nearing a gallop, pulled a rickety wooden hay cart with two men, a woman, and a child, all wrapped together in a ragged blanket of broadcloth. The child stared at Gabriel with coal-ash eyes and coughed, his body convulsing with the effort. Blood trickled from the corner of his mouth as his tiny body bounced violently along the muddy street, but his face was expressionless.

Gabriel walked for another eternity, and another, through the deserted streets of Vieux Manan, winding past bolted houses and shuttered windows in a pattern known only to a fevered lover on the verge of madness, or perhaps even already crossed over into madness. Each step drained another measure of energy from Gabriel's life-weary gait, each empty street corner stealing from his soul.

The wanderer's pace slowed, step by excruciating step, until outside a row of closely built town houses across from the harbor, rickety and weathered from this storm and years of others, the weary Gabriel finally exhaled the last of his energy and crumpled onto the soft ground, his knees buckling over his ankles and his body fluttering slowly downward, gently to the ground, like a page torn and tossed into the wind from atop a seaside bec.

He settled silently into the mud.

Alone.

eva

I close Gabe's notebook and look around. I am still on the floor of the emergency room, alone except for a nurse at the intake desk.

I get up and, brushing off my jeans, walk over to the counter. "That boy who just came in," I say to the woman behind the desk. "He was bleeding. Where did they take him?"

"I'm sorry," says the nurse. She's wearing wide, green-rimmed glasses with stems that start at the bottom of the frame and snake upward over her ear. "What boy?"

"They just took him in there." I point at the swinging doors.

"I've been at the desk for two hours. I haven't seen any

boy come through here. I haven't seen anyone at all, except for you sitting there on the floor."

"He was bleeding," I say again, my voice tinny and shallow.

She pushes back from the low desk, the wheels on the bottom of her chair squeaking as she foot-powers herself across the small office space to a file caddy, where she sifts through a short stack of files. "What did you say the name was?"

"Gabriel."

"That's his last name?" she says.

"It's Lejeune. Gabe Lejeune," I say.

"Lejeune. Lejeune. Here he is. Let's see. Emergency splenectomy." She lowers her glasses and scans the file, her polished fingernail sweeping along the bottom of the chart. "He should be in post-op," she says, glancing at her wristwatch. She slaps the file closed. "Only family can see him now." She closes the file. "Is he your boyfriend, sweetie?"

"I—" I mumble. He is not my boyfriend. He is so much more. "Is he going to be OK?" I ask.

"They will give us a prognosis after he wakes up. But in the meantime only family can see him." She readjusts her glasses over her eyes.

"What's a splenectomy?" I say.

"It's when they take your spleen out."

"Why would they do that?" I say.

eva

"Oh, there could be a million reasons. One guy came in last week after a rough hockey game and had to have his removed. It could be drugs. There was a woman last year who had some kind of cancer. Leukemia, I think. It could be anything. It's pretty common."

I hear what she's saying, but none of the words really explain anything at all. All I know is that Gabe is in trouble and in pain, and I want to help him but I'm not family, so I'm not allowed to see him even though I know him better than anyone in his so-called family does. I doubt his father even knows that Gabe is in Maine, let alone in the hospital.

I'm not crying, but I sniffle like I'm about to.

"Is he going to be OK?" I say.

The nurse looks at me over her glasses and smiles softly. "Don't worry, sweetie," she says. "Everything will be all right. He'll probably live forever."

Gabriel

"OVER HERE!" THE GIRL'S SHOUTS TORE INTO Gabriel's ears and brain. He could see nothing. "Over here!" she shouted again.

Gabriel found the will to pry his eyes open, and the sunlight, though low and muted in the steady, slowly falling rain, poured in as if for the first time. He blinked and squinted into the sky, straining to accept the muted light into his dilated eyes. He was on his back, staring upward, brown boarded buildings of Vieux Manan framing a sky of indefinite, infinite gray, cloud over cloud, circling lazily in the salty sky.

Into his sight came, suddenly and without presage, Evangeline, his life's desire, pale and thin and anguished, but alive. And here. Evangeline! Cloaked in a Cadian cape of cornflower blue, the hood drenched and dripping around her frantic, freckled skin, midnight eyes darting from point to point on his face. The stiff, white collar around her neck stood out against the gray sky, reflecting light onto her skin, the light of a sister of mercy, a wandering caregiver, his once and future beloved.

Was it a dream?

"Help us!" she shouted, to whom he could not discern. He felt himself slipping, straining to stay awake. His body, so cold in the mud a minute ago, was now numb, and he felt no discomfort.

225

"Gabriel," Evangeline said over her crumpled lover, tears welling heavily in her eyes. "At last." She bent to kiss him with colorless lips.

And as her lips met his, the young lovers, though the months and journeys had stolen from their beauty, were again, for a moment, enrobed in the golden light of Pré-du-sel, and for a moment he was grateful, alive again.

Gabriel closed his eyes, and for a moment recalled the first time Evangeline stood over him, with her hoe at his neck and Poc growling nearby. He remembered the liquid sunlight that crawled over that sylvan-bordered bec, illuminating the rolling tides of Glosekap Bay. He imagined Evangeline tending to her garden and orchards, visiting the woods to collect honey for breakfast and wildflowers for the table, her flowing black hair and ocean-blue kirtle catching the gusts, soft and aromatic with sea and meadow and peacefulness. He revisited his hiding place just beyond the wall, that concealed corner of the birch grove where he spent so much of his camouflaged youth, watching, waiting, hoping for a glimpse of her, not with malice or any intent other than love, true love, and his compulsion to sketch her, to capture her beauty that he might carry it with him. Gabriel, behind closed eyelids, saw his birchbark and charcoal sketches of Evangeline, each revealing itself in succession, here as a child among the clam beds, here as a young woman attending her chores, here as a beauty, a radiant, heavenly beauty awaiting her love, Gabriel.

"Help!" cried Evangeline. "Help us!" A window opened above them, then slammed shut.

"My beloved," he strained to say, but he was unsure if the words ever took the form of sound, or if only his lips, or his mind, expressed them. "My beloved." He opened his shivering eyes.

She was there. This was not a dream. In this moment, she was crouched against him, sheltering him from the rain, a nurse holding his troubled head in her generous hands, feeding him life. "Worry not, Gabriel. I am here now. We are together again. I will take you home."

Home, Gabriel thought to himself.

"I have waited," Evangeline whispered, leaning over Gabriel's head to brush the sodden hair from his muddy, hail-battered face. She rubbed the water from her own eyes, leaving streaks across her cheeks, breathing and rocking back and forth slowly, rhythmically. She looked down into him with fearful eyes, swallowing a sob with a weak smile, the kind of smile a mother gives to a dying child to strengthen his spirit, at the expense of her own. "I have waited for you, Gabriel."

Through the quieting rain, Gabriel could just hear the sound, so familiar to him, of the ocean tide as it turned away from the seawall across the street. He knew the speech of the tides. He understood them. He listened to the waves, less insistent by the moment, as the water retreated out to the sea, slowly, slowly drawing the strength of the storm with it.

Soon the skies would clear.

Gabriel strained to look up at his beloved, so long-sought was she, but his eyelids fluttered closed again and he went back to the bec above the village of Pré-du-sel, back to watching, sketching, and loving Evangeline, reveling in her every breath and movement, back to the house he'd so carefully and exactingly built for her, back to her table, bountiful with pumpkin and salt cod and porridge, back to her orchard, collecting apples by day and lying under the stars by night, wrapped together in the same cloak she now wore, as the constant, trustworthy tide of Glosekap Bay marked the impatient days of their magical, golden world.

228

eva

I sit hopelessly in the emergency room for another forty-five minutes, waiting for I don't know what, before I remember that I work here.

I have a hospital badge.

I may not officially be assigned to the ER or the OR, but if anyone asks why I'm there, I can just play lost. After all, I'm just the lowly work-study assistant to the assistant. How could I possibly know my way around this huge hospital?

All I have to do is get past the nurse at the desk. I don't have a plan, so I wait.

I don't have to wait long. Outside the sliding glass doors, a police car screeches to a halt, lights flashing. Seconds later, an ambulance arrives. The driver and passenger jump out of the cab and race around to the back doors, which they open to reveal what appears to be an extremely old man lying on a gurney, an oxygen mask attached to his face. The cop helps the ambulance drivers unload the gurney and wheel it into the emergency room. "Cardiac arrest!" one of them shouts to the nurse before they race through the swinging doors and disappear into the same cave where Gabe is.

I look back at the ambulance, and see inside it a very old woman sitting on the bench next to where the gurney was. She's surrounded by a wall full of medical equipment—a blood-pressure monitor, an oxygen tank, a pair of defibrillator paddles. She is strapped in with seat belts over both shoulders, but she's making no attempt to unbuckle herself or get up.

I approach the ambulance. "Ma'am?" I say.

But the woman, who is at least as old as Ada was, does not answer. She is crying. She's wrapped in a fuzzy red and blue plaid robe, and she's wearing woolen socks with no shoes.

"Where are you?" she is mumbling. "Where have you gone?"

I climb into the ambulance and sit down next to her. "Ma'am?" I say.

She looks at me, her tiny, birdlike face splotched with the blue-black of sleeplessness. Her clear, tearful eyes glisten. "Where has he gone?" she asks, as if there is no other question in the world.

I take her hand. "What is your name?" I say.

"Mrs. Gage," she says. "Mrs. Henry C. Gage. Of Biddeford."

"Come with me, Mrs. Gage," I say. "We will find him. I will help you." I unbuckle her seat belts and carefully help her down from the ambulance. She is very light. Leaning on my arm, she shuffles into the emergency room. It is empty; everyone has disappeared into the back to help with the woman's husband, who is apparently having a heart attack. I grab a wheelchair. "Here," I say, locking the wheelchair's breaks with my foot. "Sit here."

"Where is he?"

"Please, Mrs. Gage." I point at the wheelchair's seat. She sits down in the wheelchair and I wheel it through the swinging doors, into the brightly lit intake room.

There is a commotion behind one of the curtains, where the doctors are working on Mr. Gage, working to restart his stalled heart. "Clear!" shouts one voice. An electric surge pulses through the room as the paddles come down with a *clack*. I jump, but Mrs. Gage does not move.

I wheel her over to one corner of the room next to a short bench. I sit with her for a moment. I take hold of her hand while we listen to the doctors talking behind the curtain. "Clear!" one shouts, and there's another surge. I jump again.

I look over at Mrs. Gage. She is asleep.

I put Mrs. Gage's hand back in her lap and stand up. She'll be fine now. She's in a room full of doctors, and Da' always says that if someone's asleep, you shouldn't wake them. A soul has enough trouble finding rest in this world, he says.

So I let her sleep. I know that all she really wants is to be with him anyway. Whatever happens, whether he lives or dies, she just wants to be with him. I've helped her as much as I can.

Besides, I'm behind the swinging doors now, that much closer to Gabe.

Gabriel

THE LAST THING GABRIEL SAW WAS EVANGELINE'S
softly smiling face, illuminated with the blissful aura of their
youth. Her expression of devotion enveloped him in her
warmth.

Gabriel closed his tired eyes, and Evangeline laid herself
next to him in the mud, under the gray-black skies of Vieux
Manan. She kissed his lips, her arms wrapping him in
restfulness and certainty.

"My beloved," she whispered.

eva

It takes under a minute to find Gabe's room, and even less than that to slip in and close the door behind me.

He is lying in a bed, tilted partway up. His head falls to one side. His right forearm is turned outward and bent slightly back on a raised pillow to reveal his pale white inner elbow, punctured by two tubes and spotted with green and black bruises. His breathing is awkward, haphazard, and I can tell that Gabe is in pain.

My heart stings.

There is a lamp next to his bed, with a hospital gown draped over the shade to soften its intense fluorescent light. I sit down on one of the padded chairs next to the window and wait.

eva

The night outside the window is dark, and windy, and wet. This rain will turn to sleet by morning.

"You are here," Gabe says softly, without turning his head upright, without even opening his eyes. "Evangeline."

I am silent for a moment before I answer. "Yes," I say. "I am here."

He opens his eyes and gives a slight smile.

And in an instant, I am awash in unexpected anger.

For as many times as I'd rehearsed what I'd say when I saw him again, I am stuck without words. I never pictured it this way. But here, now, in a hospital room where the only person I'll ever be able to love lies ill, maybe dying, I am furious.

I want to yell at him. I want to hit him. But I don't have the words or the strength for either, so I simply turn away from him. "I'm leaving." I walk toward the door.

"Please," he says. "Evangeline." I know he is in pain. I hear it.

I stop at the door, close my eyes, and inhale. "Where were you?" I say. I insist.

"Nowhere far," he says. "I was never far. I was always nearby. In Franktown, in Brewster, in Portland. I've been waiting."

"For what?" I demand, steely and stiff-necked. "Why didn't you come to me?"

He doesn't answer.

"I memorized those woods looking for you. I could have died on that cliff you disappeared over."

He is still silent.

"Louise told me to give up on you. I even told myself to give up on you!"

"I thought you would understand," he says, interrupting. "I was lost."

"Lost?" I say. "You weren't lost. You knew exactly how to get home."

"Home?" he says. "Where is that?"

I don't say anything.

"My brother is dead," he says. "My father is gone. My mother was never here." He sighs. "Where is my home?"

I know the answer before he even asks the question, but at first I don't say it. I am afraid to. Then I think about that day under the dock, when I didn't tell him how I really felt, that I'd follow him anywhere, forever, and if only I'd said so then, maybe we would have found a way to grow up together instead of apart.

"With me," I say.

"What?"

"Your home is with me," I say. "You belong with me."

I wait for Gabe to say that I am right, to say that he is

sorry. That he will never disappear again. I want him to ask me to stay with him, forever.

But Gabe doesn't say a word.

I carry the notebook over to him and toss it on his chest. "This is yours." I turn toward the door, hoping I make it out of the room before my tears, now transforming from angry to desperately, desperately sad, take over. I fear this is the end, now, that all my searching, waiting, loving has been for nothing.

238

As the outgoing tide of Vieux Manan receded to its lowest ebb, Evangeline inhaled Gabriel's final breath. It filled her with peace.

And Gabriel's anxious heart fell quiet at last.

eva

H e dies in the end, you know," Gabe says before I can reach the door to leave his hospital room. I stop and turn to look at him. His eyes are still closed, his head resting off to the side, but his hand is now holding his notebook to his chest, pressing it against his heart.

I nod. "I know."

And then the tears come again. Tears of exhaustion, of shared pain, of separation, of togetherness. Tears that belong to Gabe and me. I don't want Gabe to die, too. Not like Ada. Not like Paul. Not like Gabriel. Not now. Not ever. I stand and stare through my tears at Gabe.

Gabe lifts his head at last and looks at me, ocean-blue eyes soft and weary. But alive. He opens the notebook. He flips to the final page. And then he rips out the page, holds it up for me to see, crumples it into a ball, and tosses it onto the floor. "It doesn't have to happen that way, Evangeline."

I don't answer.

"Come home," he says, holding up his arms. "Please, come home."

I decide, then and there, that Ada was right. My search for Gabe was never in vain, because we are now, both, finally home. Whatever the future holds for us, whatever threatening ships sail into the harbor and threaten to split us apart, our story is still being written.

It's not over.

I crawl into Gabe's bed and curl up under his blanket, pressing my ear to his chest. I listen to his steady, even heart.

"My beloved," I say.

Epilogue

LOOK AROUND.

You are alone at the top of the bluff. The distant dawn creeps up over the edge of the cliff, illuminating the meadow in a misty morning haze. The low, thorny bramble bushes and swaying sea grasses of green and gold are draped in a many-hued glow. The sun lifts over the sea, slowly but certainly, sharpening the light and revealing layers of emerald and amber and fiery scarlet as every season, every story converges on this place.

You've slept here, on this rock-altar, coddled by the far-off rumble of the waves, insistent and crashing at twilight as the tide pressed forward, but meeker now as morning takes hold and the waters recede.

A twig snaps in a glade of birch trees. You turn. Is that a shadow concealed in the wood? A deer? A man? A ghost?

The sea breeze, salty and pure and whispering, fills your lungs and mind with memories you haven't formed yet. You inhale deeply. The yellow wood lilies at the edge of the forest beckon you back to the path in the woods, back through the pines, back to your old life.

You wonder how long you've been here, and worry how you'll get home.

Another breath, deeper now, and your anxious heart slows again. You are not alone. Many have disappeared down this path, struggled, and found their way home again. Many stories surround you.

Perhaps you will linger here atop the bec awhile longer, lying on your back and tracing the sun's path against the sky, and waiting, watching, listening, hoping for the return of the distant tide.

AUTHOR'S NOTE

This we know for sure: In 1755 the French-speaking Acadian community in and around Nova Scotia was, under long-standing orders from the British crown, forcibly removed from their lands and dispersed across the Atlantic, from Maine to Argentina. Many were sent to France. The largest group of displaced Acadians settled in Louisiana. Their descendants—the Cajuns—still live there.

A hundred years later, Henry Wadsworth Longfellow heard a story from his friend Nathaniel Hawthorne about a young Acadian couple separated during the expulsion. According to the story, this couple searched for years before finally finding each other—just in time for one of them to die. It's unclear whether the story was true or invented—what's certain is that it was compelling.

Longfellow spent ten years turning the tale into his epic poem "Evangeline," a bestseller in its day. It became so popular that for many, "Evangeline" is seen as history rather than romance, something Longfellow surely never intended. But while scholars and history enthusiasts argue over the authenticity of Longfellow's interpretation, the story remains strong. Because in the end, it's not a story about Acadians, it's a story about people—about separation and reunion, about the search for what's disappeared, about devotion and hope and love.

"Evangeline" remains an unbeatable inspiration—both for me and for Gabe Lejeune, the scribbling, floppy-haired boy from Franktown who disappears, the boy Eva refuses to give up on.

The poem recounted by the notary Leblanc on pages 71–74 is excerpted from Part 1 of "Evangeline."

The words Gabe sings on page 59 are from "Vincent," by Don McLean.

The song on the car radio on page 51 is "Over the Hills and Far Away," by Led Zeppelin.

ACKNOWLEDGMENTS

Thanks are due to gentle, brilliant, beautiful Tamar Brazis, who is much smarter than I am, just as editors should be. To Maria Middleton and Chad Beckerman, who attend so carefully to every design they create. Jonathan Beckerman, for his beautiful photographs. Scott Auerbach, for his clarity and helpfulness. Jason Wells, for unyielding energy. Susan Van Metre and the team at Amulet, for believing that a centuries-old love story was worth telling again. To Dan Mandel, for helping with the p's and q's. To my friends for graciously allowing me to insert Longfellow quotations into conversation, even when they didn't belong. To A, for patience. And to Gabriel and Evangeline, for never giving up.

ABOUT THE AUTHOR

TUCKER SHAW, who has been featured on *The Today Show*, is the author of *Everything I Ate* and many popular books for teens, including *Confessions of a Backup Dancer* and *The Girls*. He lives in Denver, where he is a food editor for the *Denver Post*.

This book was designed by Maria T. Middleton and art directed by Chad W. Beckerman. The text is set in 12-point Adobe Garamond, a typeface originally drawn by the sixteenth-century French engraver and punch cutter Claude Garamond. The display font used for Gabriel is P22 Roanoke Script, and the display font used for Eva is Filosofia Unicase. The title typography is hand-drawn, based on the letter forms of Adobe Garamond.

KEEP READING!

TROY HIGH
by Shana Norris

THE GIRLS
by Tucker Shaw

BLISS
by Lauren Myracle

ANXIOUS HEARTS
by Tucker Shaw